DEATH OF A GROOM

The Hamish Macbeth series

Death of a Gossip
Death of a Cad
Death of an Outsider
Death of a Perfect Wife
Death of a Hussy
Death of a Snob
Death of a Prankster
Death of a Glutton
Death of a Travelling Man
Death of a Charming Man
Death of a Nag
Death of a Macho Man
Death of a Dentist
Death of a Scriptwriter
Death of an Addict
A Highland Christmas
Death of a Dustman
Death of a Celebrity
Death of a Village
Death of a Poison Pen
Death of a Bore
Death of a Dreamer
Death of a Maid
Death of a Gentle Lady
Death of a Witch
Death of a Valentine
Death of a Sweep
Death of a Kingfisher
Death of Yesterday
Death of a Policeman
Death of a Liar
Death of a Nurse
Death of a Ghost
Death of an Honest Man
Death of a Green-eyed Monster
Death of a Traitor
Death of a Spy
Death of a Smuggler

DEATH OF A GROOM

M.C. Beaton

with R.W. Green

CONSTABLE

CONSTABLE

First published in Great Britain in 2026 by Constable

Copyright © M. C. Beaton, 2026

1 3 5 7 9 10 8 6 4 2

The moral right of the author has been asserted.

*All characters and events in this publication, other than
those clearly in the public domain, are fictitious
and any resemblance to real persons,
living or dead, is purely coincidental.*

All rights reserved.
No part of this publication may be reproduced, stored in a
retrieval system, or transmitted, in any form, or by any means,
without the prior permission in writing of the publisher, nor be
otherwise circulated in any form of binding or cover other than that
in which it is published and without a similar condition including this
condition being imposed on the subsequent purchaser.

A CIP catalogue record for this book
is available from the British Library.

ISBN 978-1-40872-274-9

Typeset in Palatino by Initial Typesetting Services, Edinburgh
Printed and bound in Great Britain by Clays Ltd, Elcograf S.p.A.

Papers used by Constable are from well-managed forests
and other responsible sources

Constable
An imprint of
Little, Brown Book Group
Carmelite House
50 Victoria Embankment
London EC4Y 0DZ

The authorised representative
in the EEA is
Hachette Ireland
8 Castlecourt Centre
Dublin 15, D15 XTP3, Ireland
(email: info@hbgi.ie)

An Hachette UK Company
www.hachette.co.uk

www.littlebrown.co.uk

*For the whole Harding clan –
Colin, Isabella, Sofia, Bear, Chris, Hanka and Otto –
with huge thanks for always being ready
to take on Ossi.*

Foreword

I always like to say that there's an element of truth in any Hamish Macbeth escapade. The characters, of course, are entirely fictitious, as is their home village of Lochdubh, but there are always places round about, places Hamish may visit or where part of the action happens, that are real. I think that including real places helps to 'locate' Lochdubh in Sutherland, which, in turn, helps to make the characters and scenarios more believable for the reader. It certainly helps me to set the right sort of tone when I'm writing.

For me, playing with Scottish folklore is also something that adds an authentic flavour to a Hamish Macbeth tale. We Scots are famously practical and pragmatic people, a nation of engineers and inventors. Think of Alexander Graham Bell, who invented the telephone; John Logie Baird, known as 'The Father of Television'; Robert Watson-Watt and his work on radar; and, of course, Scotty from *Star Trek*. There is an enduring image of the Scots as highly intelligent, well-educated scientists and technical innovators.

That, however, is just one of the many conceptions that have become Scottish stereotypes. Another is of the anxiously superstitious Highlanders living in eerie isolation out in the wilds of the far north, on the windswept moors or in glens closed in by steep mountain slopes and swirling mists or glowering grey skies. You can understand why the atmosphere conjures superstition and tales told late at night of mystical creatures that haunt the darkness.

Like all stereotypes, those applied to the Scots are nonsense, but nonsense that might have a grain of truth, just like stereotypes of anyone else. Scots are no different than any other people, and just as different as all other people. Every culture has its traditional myths and legends, whether they involve dragons and sea serpents, witches or giants. Scotland has all of those and more.

There are hundreds of Scottish myths and legends involving giants, kelpies, selkies, goblins, brownies, fairies or witches, and *Death of a Groom* has its very own witch story, featuring Jenny Horne. Jenny, or Janet, Horne was a name given to any suspected witch in the far north and the element of truth in our little piece of Lochdubh folklore is that the last person in Britain to be legally tried and executed for witchcraft was Janet Horne, who was sentenced to be burnt at the stake in Dornoch in 1727. The unfortunate woman was probably in the throes of some form of dementia and her daughter suffered from a deformity in her hands and feet. The rumour grew that Janet had her daughter shod at night by the Devil himself so that she could ride her around the countryside as if she were a pony. She could then cover vast distances using her witch's powers to perform dastardly deeds at the Devil's bidding.

Both Janet and her daughter were arrested, although the younger woman somehow managed to escape from custody and flee the area. The unfortunate Janet stood trial and was declared guilty of witchcraft. She was smeared with tar and paraded through the streets to the spot where a bonfire had been prepared for her execution. She is said to have smiled and warmed herself by the flames that would end her life. To this day a stone stands on that very spot in Dornoch, marking the site of the demise of the last witch.

In the hills outside Lochdubh, *Death of a Groom* also features a place called the 'Spaniard's Leap'. Many will, no doubt, recognise this as a version of the Soldier's Leap at Killiecrankie, just north of Pitlochry in Perthshire. This is the spot where, in 1689, following a particularly brutal, bloody battle between government troops and Jacobite rebels, the government army was routed. One soldier, fleeing for his life from clansmen who were in hot pursuit, escaped by jumping from one rocky bank of the River Garry to the other. I've been there and it's a huge gap. I wouldn't fancy trying to jump it myself but, on the other hand, the thought of being hacked to death by bloodthirsty Highlanders with claymores might well have turned me into an Olympic long-jumper, too!

Lochdubh's Spaniard was in a slightly different predicament, but the idea that a Spaniard should be at large on the shores of northwest Scotland in 1588 isn't so far-fetched. As described in the following pages, the Spanish famously did send an armada to invade England at that time and some of the ships were wrecked off the west coasts of Scotland and Ireland.

One ship, the *San Juan de Sicilia*, put in to Tobermory Bay on the Isle of Mull and was welcomed, the Scots at that time being no friends of the English. The captain negotiated with the local clan chief, Lachlan Maclean of Duart, for supplies which Maclean agreed to arrange provided that he could borrow some of the Spanish soldiers. He then spent weeks ravaging the territories of rival clans. The ship then exploded while at anchor, killing everyone on board. It's believed that one of those providing supplies was actually an English agent. Some of the Spaniards who were not on board when the ship was blown to bits remained in Scotland for a time before being given safe passage back to Spain. Some may have settled and never left at all. The wreck of the *San Juan de Sicilia* has been the focus of several treasure-hunting salvage attempts and the notion that a fortune in Spanish gold lies at the bottom of Tobermory Bay persists to this day.

There is, therefore, an element of truth in Hamish's story about the Spaniard's Leap, although the Lochdubh version doesn't end quite so well for the Spaniard as the Killiecrankie version did for the soldier.

Given that this visit to Lochdubh features a Highland wedding in a romantic castle surrounded by glorious scenery, you might well be wondering whether Hamish and his long-term girlfriend, Claire, will get caught up in the moment and tie the knot themselves. Surely all that romance in the air – especially as the wedding is on Valentine's Day – will inspire Hamish to pop the question, won't it? He has to get married sometime, after all, doesn't he? Or does he? You'll just have to wait and see!

R. W. Green, 2026

The Wedding of Miss Alannah Hamilton and Mr Darius Palmerston

Principal Guests at the Tommel Castle Hotel (compiled by Silas Dunbar, Security Manager):

Miss Alannah Hamilton	Bride	First floor room 12
Mr Darius Palmerston	Bridegroom	Second floor room 21
Mr Charles Hamilton	Father of the Bride	First floor room 11
Mrs Serena Hamilton	Stepmother of the Bride	First floor room 11
Miss Sloane Beaumont	Chief Bridesmaid	Second floor room 23
Miss Helen Carter	Bridesmaid	Second floor room 23
Mr Sebastian Chalmers	Best Man	Second floor room 21
Mr Robert Jensen	Godfather to the Bride	First floor room 13
Viscount Carsely (Richard Wade)	Family Friend	Second floor room 25
(The Hon.) Simon Derringer	Family Friend	Second floor room 25
Mr Stephen Palmerston	Cousin of the Groom	Top floor room 33
Mr Henry Poulter	Cousin of the Groom	Top floor room 33
Mr Paul Hunter	Horse Groom	Stable block bedsit

Chapter One

To see her is to love her,
And love but her forever;
For nature made her what she is,
And never made anither!
   Robert Burns, 'O Saw Ye Bonie Lesley' (1792)

'This wedding cannae go ahead! There must be no marriage in this place! There is evil afoot – an evil no' seen for five centuries past! The ceremony will summon the Devil himself and Satan will bring death to Lochdubh!'

The old man stood in a patch of sunshine beside a low snowbank that was liberally speckled with gravel, gathered when the snow was cleared from the car park of Lochdubh's Tommel Castle Hotel. He punctuated his proclamation by pounding the tambourine-like Celtic bodhrán drum he held in his left hand, although he had no need of the drum to attract the attention of those standing at the foot the stone steps leading up to the hotel's grand entrance. His appearance had the small group rapt, none showing any inclination to retreat inside where warming log fires were burning in the public rooms. Outside, despite the sharp glare that had encouraged some of the guests to protect their eyes with designer shades, the sunshine had barely raised the temperature far enough above freezing to melt the frost on the trees. Nevertheless, the hotel guests – a handful of young women accompanied by a couple of young men – remained out in the cold, fascinated by the apparition with the drum.

The man standing before them wore a black velvet skull cap decorated with embroidered gold symbols that looked arcane enough possibly to be genuine runes from some long-forgotten mystic cult. His long, straggly, white beard reached down to his chest, almost concealing a string of dull black beads and his voluminous, heavy, grey kaftan had snow clinging to the hem where it had trailed on the ground. Now and again, when he raised his arms to sound the drum, the hem rose to reveal a distinctly non-mystical pair of thick-soled, warmly padded, modern snow boots.

'I'm getting married here on Saturday,' a young woman standing on the steps called out. Alannah Hamilton was wearing an expensive Fairisle wool sweater and stood with her arms folded against the cold. From her bemused smile and the twinkle in her eye, it was patently clear that she wasn't taking the old man at all seriously. 'Why do you want me to cancel my wedding? What's the Devil got to do with it?'

'The Devil has stalked the hills around Lochdubh since the beginning o' time, forever seeking souls to plunder,' the old man said, with another dramatic flourish on his drum. 'It was in this place that he took the witch Jenny Horne as his bride!'

As the storyteller rattled out an uncertain rhythm on his drum, plodding back and forth in a slow march while chanting in a low, incoherent mutter, a small man in a tweed suit appeared at the hotel entrance, pausing at the top of the steps, quite apart from the guests lower down. Colonel George Halburton-Smythe was the hotel's owner. Anger at the disturbance on his premises had drawn his face almost as tight as the knot in his regimental tie. He was joined by a younger man, wearing a dark business suit.

'I put you in charge of security, Silas!' hissed the colonel. 'You used to be a police officer – get rid of that old reprobate!'

'I think kicking him out might be a wee bit hasty, Colonel,' said Silas. 'It might not be good PR. Angus is known as "the seer" in Lochdubh and there are plenty who use him as a fortune teller and font of wisdom. It wouldn't go down at all well with the locals if we flung him out in the snow. Those who believe his auld wives' tales might think you were in league with the Devil yourself!'

Silas laughed. The colonel did not.

'So what do we do about him?' he snapped. 'We can't have him parading around here like this all day!'

'I've sent for someone who can handle Angus,' Silas said, looking down towards the driveway, 'and here he comes now.'

A silver Land Rover resplendent in the distinctive yellow-and-blue 'Battenberg' livery of Police Scotland drew to a halt at the head of the driveway, out of sight of the seer and his audience. Any noise the car made on the gravel was drowned out by an enthusiastic burst of drumming that spurred the old man into an almost energetic bout of hopping from one foot to the other. This brought a cheer from some of the guests, so he hopped some more.

Sergeant Hamish Macbeth stepped out of the Land Rover and paused to take in the spectacle. He was joined by his constable, Davey Forbes, for a few seconds before

Hamish approached the gaggle of guests, making his way around them and up the staircase, his long legs easily taking the steps two at a time. He was an imposing figure, standing well over six feet tall and with a shock of flaming red hair over which he crammed his uniform cap before greeting the colonel. A couple of the young women nudged each other, whispered and cast admiring glances in his direction, although the seer was now demanding their attention once again.

'Be warned and be gone from this place,' the seer exclaimed, 'afore murder returns to this house after five hundred years!'

'According to the history of the house, that's not possible,' said a woman with dark hair, standing next to the bride-to-be. Sloane Beaumont was Alannah's chief bridesmaid and was waving a printed sheet bearing the hotel logo. 'Tommel Castle was only built one hundred and fifty years ago, not five hundred.'

'A dwelling has stood on this spot far longer than that,' the seer assured her. 'Jenny Horne lived in a much smaller house, but it was here that the Devil and all the most abominable demons o' the underworld attended the wedding feast. They were served by two local lassies, enslaved under the sorcery of the evil witch! She turned their heads backwards so that her master wouldnae be affronted by them laying eyes upon him, and that's how they were found when their bodies were washed ashore in Loch Dubh the following day.'

'How could they see to serve anything if their heads were on backwards?' asked one of the young men, laughing. The seer glowered at him from beneath his shaggy eyebrows, sniffed and silenced the laughter with a rattle of his drum.

'The villagers had long suspected Jenny Horne o' witchcraft and gathered to march on her house. She warned them to leave her be, lest she call for her husband to rain fire on the village, but they threw her into the cellar beneath her house and locked her there until the sheriff's men could be summoned from Golspie.

'For two days and nights she screamed and wailed down in the cellar such that the men guarding the house could scarce hear anything else. Then, on the third day, the screaming stopped. The men opened the cellar to see if she was still alive, but found no trace o' her. What they did find was a tunnel, wi' walls as smooth as glass, leading out o' the cellar towards the mountains. One brave soul set foot in the tunnel and barely escaped wi' his life when the whole thing collapsed. You can follow the route the tunnel took to this day if you look just ower there.'

He pointed to a gulley that ran from the edge of the hotel grounds across the surrounding estate to where the mountains, white with snow, looked down over the village. He then resumed his shuffling, hopping dance as the guests clapped in time to the beat of his drum.

'I want him out of here immediately,' the colonel seethed, glaring at Hamish. 'He's trespassing and surely disturbing the peace! Can't you just arrest him?'

'Och, there's easier ways to deal wi' Angus,' Hamish replied. He took off his hat and waved it above his head, catching the dancing seer's eye. He then cupped his hand to his mouth in a drinking motion, before pointing to the back of the hotel. The seer gave an almost imperceptible nod, then addressed his audience once more.

'You've had fair warning,' he said. 'Choose not to heed my words and you will bring death to this place!'

He then headed off round the hotel, a smattering of applause seeing him on his way.

'Silas, maybe you should go and see Freddy in the kitchen,' Hamish suggested. 'I've no doubt a bit o' lunch and a wee dram would go down well wi' the seer.'

'Wait a minute!' the colonel objected. 'This is my hotel! You can't just give away my food and drink to that old fool!'

'Angus is no fool, Colonel,' Hamish said, keeping his voice low. 'Eccentric, aye, and a charlatan no doubt, but you might want to listen to this lot afore you pass judgement on him.'

The guests were now filing back into the hotel, heading for the warmth of the bar area.

'He was fabulous, wasn't he?' said one young woman.

'I loved his drumming,' one of men said, laughing and twiddling his hand as though wielding the seer's double-headed drumstick. 'Dum-dabbah-dum-dabbah-dum!'

'He was brilliant,' Sloane said to the bride. 'Did you have to pay extra for him, Alannah?'

'I've no idea,' Alannah said, smiling. 'I bet it was something my father laid on. He's really into all that folklore stuff.'

The group breezed past in a cloud of chatter. Hamish looked at the colonel and raised his eyebrows.

'Seems like they enjoyed the performance,' he said, smiling.

'Hamish is right,' came the voice of Priscilla Halburton-Smythe, stepping towards them from the small lounge to the side of the hotel entrance. She was, as always, elegantly dressed with not a hair of her smooth blonde bob out of place. Priscilla was tall and beautiful and Hamish had once been so beguiled by her that they had become engaged, much to the colonel's disapproval. He had found the thought of having a lowly police officer as a son-in-law so degrading as to be almost unbearable. The only thing that had offended him more was when Hamish called off the engagement. That had been an almost insufferable slight and he never found out why Hamish had behaved in such a scurrilous manner. The villagers were equally confused. Hamish and Priscilla, after all, had seemed the ideal couple.

No one else, however, knew Priscilla as Hamish did. Beneath her facade of warmth and charm, Priscilla was devoid of any real affection. She revelled in the attention men showered upon her, but could offer no real love in return. Although he had long since decided that she was not the woman to spend the rest of his days with, Hamish was still entranced by her beauty, wondering almost every time he saw her what life might have been like with a more amorous, more passionate version of Priscilla.

'That was a quaint and entertaining display,' she said. 'The wedding party loved it.'

'Aye, he's quite a character is auld Angus,' Hamish said. 'I didn't realise you were up here in Lochdubh, Priscilla.'

'I got in this morning,' she replied. 'One of the bridesmaids, Helen Carter, works with me in IT down in London. I persuaded her to suggest the hotel as the wedding venue and thought I'd best be here to keep an eye on things.'

While her father owned Tommel Castle, having bought it as a private residence and been persuaded by Hamish to turn it into a hotel when he later lost a fortune through poor investments, the colonel had little to do with the day-to-day running of the place. Priscilla, along with the hotel's manager, Mr Johnson, oversaw the operation of the business. She now spent more time in Lochdubh than she did in London, since most of her IT work could easily be done from her laptop wherever she was in the world.

'Hamish, would you do me a favour, please?' she asked. 'Make sure Angus – Mr Macdonald – doesn't leave until I've had a word with him.'

'Aye, no problem,' Hamish replied. 'I was on my way down to the kitchen in any case to see what Freddy's got on the stove. Davey and I have been helping to haul sheep out o' snowdrifts all morning, so I'm fair famished.'

'Macbeth, I will not have you scrounging in my hotel kitchen!' barked the colonel. 'And as for that scoundrel, Forbes,' he turned to where the Land Rover was parked, but Davey was no longer anywhere to be seen. 'Where has he . . . ?' The colonel turned back to see Hamish disappearing through a door that led downstairs to the kitchen.

'Priscilla, you cannot allow these lazy freeloaders to eat and drink us out of business!' he whined to his daughter.

'We're lucky to have them,' Priscilla maintained. 'Don't forget that Silas was once Hamish's constable, as was Freddy. Freddy is a far better chef than we could ever have hoped to tempt here to Lochdubh and Silas is our best employee. He covers at least three jobs in the hotel. Without Hamish we wouldn't have them. In fact, without Hamish you'd have had to sell Tommel Castle for a fraction of its value, if you recall.'

'Actually, I have a very good memory, my dear,' her father replied. 'I remember, for example, the callous way he treated you when—'

'We've moved on since then, Daddy. If I can let bygones be bygones, then so can you. Now, there's something I need to do.'

Priscilla hurried off in the direction of the bar, leaving her father with an uncomfortable surfeit of unspent ire. He spotted Mr Johnson working in the office behind the reception desk and marched across the hall, confident he'd find something or other about which to berate him.

Down in the kitchen, Freddy had persuaded Silas to trade his suit jacket for an apron and help a young woman, a local who worked as his part-time assistant, to prepare a mountain of vegetables needed for that evening's dinner.

Hamish, Davey and the seer were sat at a table in the corner of the kitchen enjoying steaming bowls of Cullen skink with hunks of freshly baked bread and mugs of tea. Hamish and the seer also had glasses of whisky to hand. The seer, having started before the other two, was mopping up the last of his soup with a final swab of bread when Hamish turned to him.

'So what was all that stuff about the Devil, Angus?' he asked. 'I'm fairly sure I've no' heard that tale afore.'

'Whether you've heard it or no',' the seer assured him, 'doesn't mean it's no' true. The evidence is there to see. You cannae deny the track o' the collapsed tunnel.'

'The gulley's there, plain as day,' Davey said, 'but there are gulleys like that all over the northwest. Geologically, we're sitting on a fault line called the Moine Thrust and . . .' He looked up from his soup when he realised Hamish was staring at him, giving him a slight shake of his head. The seer scowled at the young constable.

'Macbeth probably thinks I didn't see him shutting you up,' the old man growled. 'He kens very well how unwise it is to ignore the auld ways. Folk around here live in tune wi' their surroundings. They ken the waters o' the loch, the changes in the wind and feel o' the hillsides wi' a knowledge that runs far deeper than mere science.'

The seer took a deep breath, clearly about to launch into a lecture about ancient values, when Priscilla walked into the kitchen.

'Might I have a word with you outside, Mr Macdonald?' she asked, then continued walking past the group and out of the back door to where the small courtyard area was bright with frigid sunshine. Immediately recognising the shape of the tissue-wrapped package she was carrying, the seer rose from his seat, downed what was left of his dram and followed her outside.

'That was a fascinating recital you gave us earlier,' Priscilla said, once they were alone. She held out the package. 'I thought you might like this as a small token of our appreciation.'

'You don't understand what you're dealing wi' . . .' the seer began, taking the package and peeling back a fold of the wrapping, spotting the stylised gold stag's head logo and swiftly secreting the bottle of Glenfiddich deep in a pocket somewhere in the folds of his kaftan, '. . . but your token o' appreciation is also much appreciated.'

'I was thinking,' Priscilla said, slowly, 'that the Jenny Horne story happened a very long time ago, and—'

'Five centuries have passed,' the seer intoned, as though about to launch into his sermon once again, 'yet the danger remains ever present, merely dormant, not purged, even to this day.'

'Yes, five centuries and not much in the way of purging,' Priscilla agreed, 'but there are no real records going back quite that far here in Lochdubh, are there? There are no documents stored in the church or anywhere else to prove that the two girls were found dead on the beach or that Jenny Horne was locked in her cellar – or precisely when this all happened. I mean, you can't be sure that the fifth centenary of the Devil's wedding is this coming Saturday, or in three weeks' time, or indeed a month after that.'

'The precise day will matter not if the evil should be awakened,' warned the seer.

'My point entirely,' Priscilla said, nodding. 'I'm so glad we're seeing eye-to-eye on this, Mr Macdonald. The thing is, we have another wedding coming up in three weeks and I wondered if you could be persuaded to stage a repeat performance.'

'It would be wise to offer the same warning to your new guests,' the seer agreed, carefully considering the request, 'but I am sore troubled wi' the many demands on my time.'

'Maybe this will help ease your troubles,' Priscilla said, offering him a white envelope, which the seer opened, assessing the collection of £10 notes inside with a keen, sharp glance before the envelope, like the bottle, disappeared into the folds of his kaftan.

'It would be nice, however, if we could have a happier ending next time,' Priscilla said. 'Perhaps you might be able to offer some reassurance to my guests – something to give them a little comfort rather than disturbing nightmares that will leave them in fear of being murdered in their beds.'

'I shall work hard to find a combination of words and

rituals to allay your folks' fears next time, but you must beware, Miss Halburton-Smythe. Evil is approaching Tommel Castle as we speak and death will follow. I have seen it. It will happen. Nothing can be done to stop that now.'

The seer picked up his drum from where he had left it by the back door, and strode off round the building, heading for the village. Priscilla watched him depart, mulled over what he had said and shivered, suddenly feeling a chill far deeper than the cold Highland air. She hurried back into the warmth of the kitchen.

'So what was all that business wi' Angus about?' Hamish asked as Priscilla joined the two police officers at the table. Freddy had handed her a cup of tea as soon as she walked in, although hers was in a dainty china cup rather than the mugs Hamish and Davey preferred.

'The wedding guests enjoyed his little pantomime,' Priscilla said, smiling. 'At least one even thought the bride had paid extra for him. That works well for the hotel. This wedding is important to us.'

'There's been plenty o' wedding receptions here afore now,' Hamish said. 'What's so special about this one?'

'Local weddings are great for the hotel, but Saturday's event is a far grander affair. I know these people, Hamish,' Priscilla explained. 'They have lots of money. Alannah Hamilton's father is a very successful investment banker, as was her grandfather. It's their family business. They don't do things by halves. For them, everything has to be the very best and they're spending a fortune here. Mr Johnson and I have been involved in organising absolutely everything – from the travel arrangements to the menus over the next few days and the flowers decorating the church. We've pressed the hotel's old stable block back into service because the bride will travel to and from the church in a horse-drawn carriage that belongs to the family. They've even brought their own horses and a groom to look after them.'

'It sounds like one big headache to me,' Hamish said. 'Why did they decide to come all the way to Lochdubh for the wedding? February's no' a great time to be travelling up here.'

'Their family and friends are spread all over the country and Alannah and Darius, her fiancé, wanted something special and intimate – a Valentine's Day wedding. His parents died in a car crash a few years ago and he has no close family. They didn't want the wedding to look like it was dominated by Allanah's family, so they decided to get out of London and keep it smaller, but exceptional. I persuaded them that Lochdubh was a perfect romantic setting. The church and the hotel are ideal for them. Altogether there will be about sixty in attendance. Darius will be arriving later this afternoon with his best man and a few friends. Alannah's family are due to be here shortly.'

'Well, Lochdubh couldn't look prettier for them wi' the snow on the mountains and piled up at the sides o' the roads,' Hamish said. 'We've spent the last two days making sure the roads are clear, haven't we, Davey?'

'Aye, we have,' Davey agreed, without looking up from his soup bowl. Having had a huge crush on Priscilla when he first came to Lochdubh, he now felt distinctly uneasy when she was around and had said nothing since she appeared in the kitchen.

'What's up, Davey?' she said. 'Cat got your tongue?'

'What? No ... I mean, I'm a wee bit tired, that's all,' he said, rubbing his eyes. 'I think I'll just grab some fresh air and maybe pay a visit to see those horses you mentioned.'

'He didn't seem very pleased to see me,' Priscilla said, watching Davey crossing the courtyard.

'Aye, well, I suppose he's missing Susan, his girlfriend,' Hamish said, sipping his tea. 'Your mention o' Valentine's Day wouldn't have helped. She's at the university down south in Stirling, training to be a teacher. The bad weather's meant he's no' been able to get down there lately.'

'And what about Claire, your little paramedic?' Priscilla asked with a mischievous smile. 'Is she still sending your pulse racing?'

Hamish shifted in his seat, now feeling some of the discomfort that had driven Davey out into the cold. Talking to Priscilla about Claire felt like some kind of betrayal. He and Priscilla made far better friends than lovers, but he wasn't happy about providing her with insights into his relationship with Claire. He was also perfectly aware that she was asking with the intention of winding him up.

'Aye, we're fine,' he said. 'I've no' seen much o' her just recently wi' our odd work shifts and the snow, but we're both off tonight, so that'll be braw. Are you ... um ...' he almost asked her about her own love life, then thought better of it, '... friends wi' many o' the wedding crowd, or just the bridesmaid?'

'I'm friends with a few of them,' she said, looking down at her teacup. Having been lied to by some of the most dishonest, two-faced, deceitful villains you could ever have the misfortune to meet, Hamish knew she wasn't telling the whole truth. 'They're very interesting people. I'm sure you'll get the chance to meet some of them. In fact, we might need your help with a few things...'

*

While Priscilla began running through the logistics of the biggest wedding to happen in Lochdubh since Jenny Horne got hitched to the Devil, Davey was trying and failing to phone Susan. He guessed she was in a lecture when she didn't answer. Shoving his phone back in his pocket, he headed in the direction of the stable block, where he saw the colonel's dark green Range Rover was parked. He stopped by the car when he heard hushed voices. Standing between the car and the wall of the stables, he could make out from their conversation that two people were just round the corner – a man and a woman. There was a note of desperate anguish in their voices that made him pause to listen.

'I can't believe you're going through with this,' came the man's voice. 'You know what he's like.'

'You and I both know that,' the woman's voice replied, 'but we've talked about this, Paul, and we have to stick to the plan. It's only for one day, then Daddy will take care of him. I have to go now. People will start to wonder where I am. Remember – just stick to the plan and everything will be fine.'

Realising the conversation was over, Davey took a few quick steps round the car, then shuffled his feet noisily and coughed to make it look like he'd just walked out of the hotel. He wanted to make sure the couple knew he was coming without them thinking he'd been lurking and eavesdropping, especially since that was precisely what he *had* been doing. Alannah Hamilton came round the corner of the stable block and smiled at him.

'Hello, Constable,' she said. 'What brings you out to the stables?'

'Well, umm . . . I love horses and was hoping to make friends with the ones you've brought with you,' Davey offered by way of explanation.

'Blaze and Brandy are certainly both very friendly,' she said, flashing him another smile. 'I was just checking they're settling in okay after their long journey. They have to be on their best behaviour for Saturday, but I'm sure they will be. We've had them for years and they're gentle souls. If only people could be more like horses, eh?'

'That would often make my job a lot easier,' Davey said, laughing.

'I'm starting to feel the cold,' Alannah said with a shiver. 'I'd best get inside. Paul, the groom, will show you Blaze and Brandy.'

She hurried off towards the hotel. Davey wondered for a second what they could have been talking about that had generated such emotion, who the 'he' was they had mentioned and what their plan might be. He shrugged, dismissed it as none of his business and walked round to introduce himself to Paul. The young man was lean and fit with a mop of dark, wavy hair. He shook Davey's hand with a firm grip, looking tense and worried at first but relaxing a little when Davey explained that he'd come to see the horses.

'Take a few of these,' Paul said, grinning and passing Davey a handful of Polo mints. 'I don't let them have too many, but they love them.'

Davey turned to one of the horses, a beautiful chestnut with a white flash down the middle of his face. The horse reached its head out over the stable door.

'I take it from your white patch that you're Blaze,' he said, holding a mint flat in his hand and letting Blaze gently take it. He stroked the horse's nose. 'You're a handsome, lad, aren't you? Big and strong, too.'

Clearly having heard the crunching of mints and anxious not to be left out, another horse's head appeared from the adjacent stall. Like Blaze, Brandy had a glossy chestnut coat, but his mane was a far lighter colour.

'And you must be Brandy,' Davey said, offering the horse a mint. 'You're every bit as good looking as your pal, aren't you? They must look very glamorous together pulling a carriage, Paul.'

'They do,' Paul agreed. 'You'll get a chance to see them and the carriage on Saturday.'

'Are they both fit and well after the journey up here?' Davey asked, wondering if the conversation he had heard might have been about one of the horses.

'They're in top form,' Paul said. 'Rested and raring to go.'

'Are they purely carriage horses,' Davey asked, 'or can you ride them as well?'

'They're trained for both – perfectly happy to be saddled,' Paul said. 'Alannah ... Miss Hamilton ... and I often take them for a hack around her father's estate down in Hampshire. Do you ride?'

'I've done a bit down in the Borders, where I was brought up,' Davey said. 'I haven't been in the saddle for a while, though.'

'It's something you never forget, and these two are really well behaved, clever boys – easy to train. I'd have loved the chance to try them pulling a sleigh, so it's a pity the roads are clear.'

'Don't let any of the locals hear you saying that,' Davey said, smiling. 'There's only one road into Lochdubh, and when it's blocked we're pretty much cut off. Everyone around here hates it when that happens.'

'What about the harbour?' Paul asked. 'I was taking a stroll around there yesterday. Can't people and supplies come and go by boat?'

'If there's a bad storm, boats can't get in beyond the rocks at the mouth of the loch,' Davey replied, 'and, in any case, a boat's not much good if you need to go inland, to the hospital at Braikie, for example.'

'Is Lochdubh regularly cut off?'

'Only in a really heavy snowstorm.' Davey gazed out on the surrounding hillsides, squinting against the glare to look above the forest treeline to where haughty summits, resplendent in cloaks of white snow, stood proudly against the blue sky. 'It doesn't happen very often, although Hamish, my sergeant, reckons we've not seen the last of the snow yet, and he's not usually wrong about these things.'

'That would get all of the wedding party really excited,' Paul said. 'We can go a whole winter down south and never see a single flake of snow. Lochdubh looks like a winter wonderland right now but I'm sure we all wish we could see some snow falling.'

'Be careful what you wish for,' Davey said. 'We really have our work cut out for us when there's heavy snow. It might look nice, but just because it's pretty doesn't mean it's not a killer. It can turn a simple journey into a nightmare.'

'Well, let's keep our fingers crossed for fair weather, then and . . .' Paul paused, turning his head slightly to concentrate on a noise in the far distance. The relaxed, cheerful demeanour seemed to drain from his face when he recognised the sound. 'I'd best make myself busy,' he said. 'Sounds like the boss is here.'

The noise grew into a stuttering sound that quickly

swelled to a regular rhythmic beat accompanied by the whine of a turbine engine. Davey looked out in the direction of the loch, hidden from view by the trees in the hotel grounds. Then, above the white mountain peaks, he spotted a fast-approaching helicopter. As it drew closer he could see it was painted in a deep burgundy livery, the sunshine glinting on its glossy bodywork.

Silas rushed past, wearing ski goggles and a parka. One hand clamped a mobile phone to his ear. He made his way to the flat, open space that was normally a lush, green paddock but now looked more like a white carpet, dotted here and there with deer tracks. Silas waved to the helicopter as it circled the hotel twice, the pilot assessing the paddock as a landing area. Apparently satisfied, he brought the aircraft to a hover above the snow and slowly descended. Compared with the silence that had reigned after the seer's drumming session, the din from the engine and the rotor blades was now deafening. Davey smiled when he imagined Lochdubh's residents at back doors and upstairs windows, craning their necks to see what was going on. It wasn't every day that such a machine appeared in the skies over the village.

As the helicopter sank lower, the downdraught from its rotor blades whipped the topmost layer of snow into a swirling cloud of spindrift. Silas stood his ground, the ski goggles protecting his eyes from the stinging snow. Paul had disappeared into the stables and Davey looked away from the mini-blizzard to see Priscilla and Hamish standing close by, just beyond the snow cloud, watching the landing. The helicopter's skids sank into the knee-deep snow and the cloud it had kicked up settled with the slowing of the rotors, the engine's roar gradually descending to a comparative whisper.

Silas whipped off his goggles and rushed to the colonel's Range Rover, driving out in a careful loop to park by the helicopter. He then unloaded a roll of matting from the back of the car and laid it like a welcome carpet running to the aircraft. Once it was tromped down into a firm surface, he opened the cabin door to usher three passengers out of the helicopter and into the waiting car.

'Quite an entrance, was it no'?' Hamish remarked, Davey joining him as Priscilla hurried off to be ready with the welcome party around at the hotel's main entrance.

'It was that,' Davey agreed. 'Will that be the bride's parents?'

'Apparently so,' Hamish said, watching the three passengers climb into the Range Rover. 'Priscilla said that's Charles Hamilton wi' his wife, Serena, and his best friend, who's also the bride's godfather.'

The Range Rover made stately progress across the paddock before sweeping past them once it found firmer footing on the cleared gravel closer to the hotel. It was then that Hamish spotted a fourth person disembarking from the helicopter. Although padded out in a bulky winter jacket, he recognised the figure immediately.

'Crivens!' he breathed. 'Here's a turn-up for the books!'

Elspeth Grant looked in their direction. Even at a distance, her silver-grey eyes sparkled behind the faux-fur trim on the hood of her jacket, giving her the look of a wolf stalking through the snow towards them.

'Hamish!' she cried, wrapping her arms around his chest. Like Priscilla, Elspeth had once been engaged to Hamish. Unlike Priscilla, he regretted ever having let Elspeth go. In his heart, however, he knew that they were not destined for each other. She had headed south, trading her job as a newspaper reporter in the Highlands for the irresistible opportunity to work in TV news in Glasgow. She'd since become a familiar face on screen, revelling in the hustle and bustle of life in the big city. Hamish, on the other hand, could never imagine living anywhere other than his beloved Lochdubh. He had come to accept that they wanted different things from life and that, ultimately, was what had driven them apart.

'What on earth are you doing back here?' he asked, returning her embrace. 'And arriving by helicopter, no less!'

'That's a strange story,' she said after greeting Davey with another hug. The police radio clipped to his jacket chirped and he excused himself to take the call.

'The helicopter belongs to the TV company,' Elspeth explained once she and Hamish were alone. 'That was my boss, Robert Jensen, with Mr and Mrs Hamilton in the Range Rover. He's the company chairman.'

'Couldn't they have squeezed you in?' Hamish said, laughing. 'Surely there was room for a wee one in a car that big.'

'When I spotted you, I asked to be left behind,' Elspeth said. 'I said I wanted to take a good look around the hotel to soak up the snowy atmosphere for my report.'

'They've sent you up here to do a wedding report?' Hamish could scarcely believe it. 'That's no' the sort of thing you're usually involved wi' nowadays.'

'No, it's not, but this is more than just a wedding, Hamish. My boss has been best friends with Alannah Hamilton's father since they were at school. He's Alannah's godfather. When he said he wanted someone from the station up here to cover the wedding, I was the one who sprang to mind – the local girl who knows the area.'

'Aye, when you put it like that, I suppose you couldn't really refuse.'

'Oh, I could have,' Elspeth said slowly, 'but once I started looking into those involved, I practically insisted on coming. Hamish, there's something very weird about the Hamiltons and this wedding. There are all sorts of strange stories about them – lies, deceit and sinister secrets. I have the most dreadful feeling that something truly awful is about to happen. Someone is going to die!'

Chapter Two

Nobody who has not been in the interior of a family can say what the difficulties of that family might be.
Jane Austen, *Emma* (1815)

'What do you mean, "Someone's going to die"?' Hamish asked Elspeth. 'Are you talking about your gift?'

Generations of women in Elspeth's family had been known to have 'second sight', giving them a psychic ability to see things that others could not – even things that were yet to happen.

'We've already had Angus Macdonald parading around here wi' a drum this morning predicting doom and gloom,' Hamish went on. 'You're no' telling me he was right, are you?'

'I've no idea what the seer said,' Elspeth defended herself. 'He may be a bit of a fraud at times, but he's told you things before that no one else could have known. You also know that I'm nothing like him and that—'

'Aye, aye, you're the real deal, I ken that just fine,' he said, calming her. 'I didn't mean anything by it. What is it that's been upsetting you? What have you seen?'

'A dead body,' she said, slowly, 'and a white tower, flecked with red.'

'There's no white towers around here,' he said, 'and flecked wi' red? Do you mean splattered wi' blood?'

'Perhaps . . .' she said, 'but it's not just that, Hamish, it's what I've been finding out about . . .'

'Hamish!' Davey called from the driveway at the side of the hotel. 'A car's spun off on ice up on the Strathbane road!'

'I've got to go, Elspeth,' Hamish said, settling his hands on her shoulders and looking her in the eye, 'but if there's something bothering you about these folk and this wedding, then I want to hear about it. I'll give you a call and we'll meet up later.'

She watched him trot off to catch up with Davey, then made her way into the hotel. She gave herself a shake and forced a smile. She would banish the feeling of dread to the back of her mind and get on with her job, just as she always did.

The garish fluorescent colours of the police car and the ambulance, with their blue lights flashing, looked glaringly alien against the simple white of the moors and hills, the lush green of the pine forests and the cool blue sky. Parked alongside the emergency vehicles was a small grey hatchback, and lying a little way off the road was a badly battered blue saloon.

Hamish and Davey stood beside the grey car, talking to the occupants, Davey taking their details.

'It was good of you to stop and help, Mrs Macsween,' Hamish said to the driver. 'Seeing the other car go off the road must have given you a fair fright.'

'No' half,' replied the driver, turning to her husband in the passenger seat. 'It was like something off the telly, was it no', Rab?'

'It was that, Ella,' her husband agreed. 'The car skidded right in front o' us, then shot up the snow bank and birled right ower onto its roof, then back onto its wheels. I thought they'd be deid.'

'Fortunately, they seem to have come away with just a few bumps and bruises,' Davey said, 'but they could have been stuck out here for a while if you hadn't called for an ambulance.'

'It was Ella that phoned,' the man said. 'I went clumping through the snow to see if they'd snuffed it.'

Hamish thanked the couple again for their help and sent them on their way, warning them to take care on the icy road. Davey took the now well-trodden path through the snow to the wrecked car and Claire stepped out of the back of the ambulance, leaving her partner with their patients.

'We've got one concussion and one in shock,' she told him. 'Both have some nasty bruising, but they were lucky.'

'Aye, their seatbelts and the airbags did their jobs,' Hamish said.

'We'll have to take them in to the hospital for more checks,' she said. 'Do you need a word wi' them first?'

'Aye, I'll let them know their car will bide where it is until Dougie Tennant can get here wi' his recovery truck. Davey's checking through the car for valuables and personal stuff. We'll keep everything safe for them.'

'I need to let Braikie know we're on the way in. You still okay for tonight?'

'Aye, of course!' he said, grinning. 'Davey's holding the fort so I can have a night off. Drinks in the Piper, then dinner in the Napoli!'

'See you later, then!' she said, craning her neck to

give him a quick kiss before climbing into the cab of the ambulance.

Hamish looked round at the sound of powerful engines to see a small convoy of three vehicles approaching. A few moments later the cars slowed to a halt beside him, a black Range Rover leading two large, black Mercedes SUVs. The driver's window of the Range Rover slid down and a man in a grey suit nodded a greeting.

'Everything okay here, Sergeant?' he asked. 'Anything we can help wi'?'

The accent was Scottish, but not local. He was from the south – somewhere around Glasgow, Hamish guessed.

'We've got it all sorted,' Hamish said, 'but thanks for the offer. There's plenty would just have driven by.'

'And that's what we should do, driver!' The voice came from the rear seats. The windows were blacked out but, looking past the driver, Hamish could just make out two men. The accent was English – a lazy, upper-class drawl. 'We want to try out the village pub and it will be open by now. We need to get there before the damned locals drink it dry!'

The second man let out a snort of laughter. The driver looked at Hamish, sighed and gave a slight shake of his head.

'Of course, Mr Palmerston,' he said, and the small convoy rumbled off down the road.

'Posh cars,' Claire said from the ambulance, leaning out of the cab window. 'Where are they heading?'

'I can guess,' Hamish said, watching the black cars disappearing into the distance, 'and I doubt we've seen the last o' them.'

He turned to the back of the ambulance to talk to the injured middle-aged couple, then Claire waved a farewell and departed for Braikie, leaving Hamish to help Davey secure the crashed car.

The black Range Rover led the two Mercedes down from the high road and across the old stone bridge over the River Anstey, heading into Lochdubh. They drove through the village drawing inquisitive stares from passers-by. The tourist season regularly brought expensive cars to the village, despite the single-road access making Lochdubh something of a dead end, with no way simply to 'pass through' on the way to somewhere more glamorous. At this time of year, however, with the late summer and autumn visitors but a distant memory and with the spring influx still some way off, the road was quiet, making the convoy even more conspicuous.

The three cars cruised along the shore road before turning left on reaching the gates of the Tommel Castle Hotel. By the time they had negotiated the winding driveway, a reception committee, forewarned of their arrival by phone, was waiting for them at the foot of the entrance steps. Priscilla stood ready with Silas by her side. He was clutching a clipboard and a pen, having been briefed by Priscilla on precisely who the new arrivals were. He had a detailed note about each of them in order that he could make sure all of the hotel staff, especially the temporary workers, knew with whom they were dealing. Local villagers, happy to take on a few hours' paid work, had been drafted in as extra waiters, waitresses and porters to help with the wedding over the course of the weekend.

The first passenger to fling open a door, narrowly missing the driver who was about to open it for him, was Darius Palmerston, the bridegroom. He was tall, with an athletic build, dark hair and dark eyes, his handsome face lightly bronzed with the sort of tan acquired in a ski resort. Silas ticked him off his list.

Palmerston turned to his Range Rover travelling companion, Sebastian Chalmers, and said something in a low voice. Chalmers looked in Priscilla's direction and chuckled, then Palmerston strode towards her, arms outstretched to envelop her in a hug.

'Priscilla!' Palmerston said. 'You're looking gorgeous as always!'

'Well, umm, thank you, Darius,' she replied, looking a little relieved when he stepped back and Chalmers offered a similar greeting. He wasn't quite as tall as Palmerston, he wasn't quite as handsome, his alpine tan wasn't quite as even and his hug wasn't quite as confident.

Silas put a tick beside his name. According to his notes, Palmerston and Chalmers had gone to a top-flight boarding school and then served in the army together. They'd been best friends for more than twenty years. Chalmers was to be Palmerston's best man.

There was a babble of conversation and introductions as the four passengers from the two Mercedes approached. Tallest by far – Silas estimated a little taller even than Hamish – and with hair the colour of straw, was Richard Wade, marked on the list as Viscount Carsely. A young man who had inherited a considerable fortune, he was regularly declared by columnists writing breathless updates in society magazines to be one of England's most eligible bachelors. Accompanying Wade was Simon Derringer, who was identified in brackets as 'The Honourable', although Silas wasn't entirely sure what that title actually meant. He made a mental note to look it up. The final two, who disembarked from the second Mercedes, were Stephen Palmerston and Henry Poulter, distant cousins of the groom, the only members of his remaining family daring enough to venture so far north.

Alannah Hamilton then appeared in the hotel entrance, squealing with delight and trotting down the stone stairs to greet everyone before linking arms with Darius Palmerston and giving him a peck on the cheek.

'Come inside out of the cold!' she called, hurrying back up the steps with her husband-to-be. 'Everyone's waiting for you in the bar! Priscilla will take care of the bags!'

Silas looked at Priscilla, who was watching the group of seven disappear into the hotel with a slightly bemused expression, never in her entire life having been left to 'take care of the bags'. She looked round to where two of the temporary staff, wearing green tweed, 'Tommel Castle' waistcoats, were helping the drivers unload the cars.

'Why don't you join the guests?' Silas said. 'I'll see to the luggage.'

'Thank you, Silas,' she replied, and made her way inside.

Silas supervised the unloading of the baggage and, given that the passengers from each car would be sharing twin rooms, allocated each carload to the appropriate room before helping carry the bags inside as far as the reception area. He then left the temporary porters to deliver the bags to the rooms and stationed himself near the entrance to the bar area, his clipboard tucked under his arm. He tried to be unobtrusive, almost out of sight, in order that he could make himself available should he be needed, yet not intrude on the gathering.

He looked around the main bar where the guests had gathered in small groups, drinking champagne, chatting happily and transforming the bar in a way Silas had never seen before. The bar itself was no different from usual, but the guests gave it the feel of an alpine ski hotel with most wearing the kind of warm and colourful sweaters you might see at an après-ski party. One exception was Charles Hamilton, the father of the bride. He was wearing a tweed sports jacket and checked shirt and was deep in discussion with his daughter, his old friend Robert Jensen and Priscilla.

To their left was a group of four dominated by the dark-haired Sloane Beaumont, Alannah's chief bridesmaid. Silas noticed that she had changed since coming indoors, now sporting a sweater with a snowflake motif and a plunging V-neck that showed off a glittering diamond-and-gold pendant which, when she threw her head back to laugh at something Sebastian Chalmers had said, Silas could see matched her equally impressive earrings. The other two standing with her were the bridegroom's cousins, Stephen Palmerston and Henry Poulter, who clearly weren't finding anything Chalmers had to say anywhere near as hilarious as the chief bridesmaid seemed to think.

Elspeth appeared to be working the room, drifting from one group to another, and was currently occupied with Viscount Carsely, who also had a couple of the other female wedding guests hanging on his every word.

Silas watched Darius Palmerston enter from the dining room along with Serena Hamilton, the bride's stepmother. To Silas, the two women looked more like sisters, Serena only a few years older than Alannah. Both had blonde hair and both were stunningly attractive, although Serena relied a little more on her make-up for her glamorous image. She had gone for the après-ski look in a Norwegian, black-and-white, stylised rose-pattern sweater, black leggings and black leather ankle boots with heels as high as a snowdrift.

Observations such as those he was making, Silas mused, were what should have made him a good police officer. Unfortunately, he had been hopelessly ill-suited to almost every other aspect of the job. All things considered, he was far happier working at the hotel.

He wondered for a second why Serena and Darius were coming from the dining room but assumed they had been familiarising themselves with the layout ahead of the big day on Saturday. Any further thoughts Silas might have had were interrupted by the insistent tinkling of Priscilla tapping a teaspoon against her champagne glass to attract everyone's attention.

'Good afternoon, everyone,' she said, loud enough to silence the last whispers of persistent chatter. 'I believe we're all here now.' She looked towards Silas, who glanced at his list and nodded. 'I would like to welcome you all to Tommel Castle. I hope those of you who have just arrived aren't too exhausted from the long journey . . .'

She went on to let them know that a buffet lunch would be served shortly in the dining room and that they could relax in the hotel or the grounds that afternoon, or take a walk into the village to enjoy the beautiful surroundings of Lochdubh.

'It looks like the weather will stay fine tomorrow,' she said, 'so for those of you who would like a more challenging walk, a local guide will take us on a hike into the hills where we can seek out the indigenous wildlife and do a bit of deer spotting.'

'Are we stalking?' asked Wade. 'I'd have brought along a hunting rifle if I'd known.'

'No shooting, Dickie,' Alannah insisted. 'I don't want people out in the hills slaughtering the local wildlife the day before my wedding.'

'No, of course not,' the viscount replied, giving her a broad smile. Only his close friends called him 'Dickie' and he was proud to count her among the closest. 'We're all here to celebrate and I wouldn't dream of spoiling your big day.'

'As an alternative,' Priscilla said, 'we've arranged for a local fisherman to take a party out on the loch for a spot of fishing.'

'So it's okay for us to murder fish but not to shoot deer?' Palmerston asked, looking at his fiancée with a lopsided grin. 'Don't fish count as "local wildlife"?'

'Fishing's different,' Alannah said, defiantly. 'You can always throw the fish back.'

'Ah, so we're just going to torment the poor things,' Palmerston said, chuckling. 'Maybe we could be kinder to them and shoot the fish!'

He laughed, as did Chalmers, but a heavy silence blanketed the rest of the room.

'Why are you being so awkward?' Alannah said. 'I just want everyone to have a nice time. Of course you can keep the fish you catch. It's totally not the same as . . .'

'What sort of catch might we take at this time of year?' asked Derringer, keen to move the discussion along.

'I can answer that,' said the colonel, walking in from the reception area. 'I might even join you tomorrow. We can hope for salmon, but there are also cod, haddock and ling if we drop our lines deep enough. Archie Maclean, the fisherman, knows all the best spots out near the mouth of the loch.'

'Excellent!' said Palmerston, rubbing his hands and looking towards the viscount. 'We might even have a little wager on the best catch, eh, Dickie?'

'You're on!' Wade replied, laughing, although looking a little uncomfortable with Palmerston using the pet name. 'I'll wager that you couldn't catch a cold!'

There was a ripple of polite laughter before Priscilla called their attention once more.

'Dinner this evening will be black tie, as per your invitations,' she said. 'We will gather here in the bar for cocktails at seven.'

The guests returned to their conversations and a waiter and waitress circulated to top up their champagne. Alannah stood in front of Darius, her eyes narrowed, her jaw set firm. She spoke in a voice too hushed for her guests to hear, but with a clipped delivery that made her anger patently clear. Silas witnessed the confrontation, shrinking back behind a tall plant stand supporting a large, potted aspidistra, to make himself all but invisible.

'Did you have to embarrass me like that?' Alannah said, clutching her champagne in one fist and clenching the other by her side.

'I think you're overreacting a bit, princess,' he said, looking down into her face. 'It was just a bit of fun.'

'Fun?' she repeated. 'Sometimes your idea of fun can be anything *but* fun, you know that? You were demeaning and you humiliated me in front of our guests! You're going to have to learn how to behave!'

'I will behave in whatever way I please,' he said, with a cold smile. 'You, on the other hand, are going to have to—'

She turned her back on him and stomped off to join Sloane Beaumont, adopting a convincing expression of carefree frivolity as she did so. Palmerston looked round, perhaps expecting to find Chalmers at his elbow, but encountering Charles Hamilton instead.

'You have a lot to learn, young man,' Hamilton said, gravely.

'About Alannah?' Palmerston replied. 'I think we know how each other tick.'

'Not just about Alannah,' Hamilton said, 'and I seriously doubt if you yet know anything about how best to keep my daughter happy. No, you need to learn how to treat people in a decent manner. You'll have to deal with people who can be far more difficult than Alannah when you're part of the family firm.'

'I know and I'm sorry, Charles,' Darius said, clearly realising that he was risking incurring the wrath not only of his future father-in-law but also his future employer. 'I'll apologise to Alannah and make it up with her, too, of course. I was being crass and out of character but I didn't mean it to sound that way. I was just trying to jolly things along, really.'

'Don't disappoint me, Darius,' warned Hamilton. 'You've got too much at stake now and I have very little patience with anyone who crosses me.'

Just as his daughter had done, Hamilton then left Palmerston standing alone. The younger man immediately caught the eye of his best man, Sebastian Chalmers, and called him over.

'Seb, as soon as we've grabbed a bite to eat,' he said, 'if there's anything worth eating in this dump, round up some of the chaps. I feel like a bit of fresh air and it's high time we paid a visit to that local pub.'

*

Hamish and Davey drove along the shore road towards Lochdubh police station with Davey at the wheel. Sitting in the passenger seat gave Hamish more of a chance to enjoy the view out over the loch. The water was so still it looked like it might have frozen solid, although that had never been known to happen. Despite the fact that he had seen it thousands of times before, the spectacle of mountains and sky reflected in the water still captivated him. He doubted his eyes would ever tire of drifting over the landscapes around Lochdubh. The idyllic scene was interrupted by the now familiar roar of a turbine engine and the dark red helicopter appeared. Davey stopped the car and they watched the aircraft skim low across the water before climbing at the head of the loch and turning south.

'The chopper didn't stay long,' Davey said, watching it disappear over the mountains.

'Priscilla said it was needed elsewhere today,' Hamish replied. 'An expensive beast like that needs to work hard to earn its keep.'

Davey was about to drive on but left his foot covering the brake when his eyes turned to the road only to see two elderly ladies standing directly in front of the Land Rover. They wore identical green woollen hats which, with the earflaps down against the cold, almost entirely contained their tightly permed grey hair. Each sported a pair of large-framed spectacles, a beige camel-hair coat buttoned up to the neck, a brown leather handbag and fur-lined boots that zipped up the front.

'The Currie twins,' Hamish sighed, knowing he had no choice but to engage with Lochdubh's two most utterly respectable residents. 'Crivens, now we're in trouble, Davey. What do these two want?'

He got out of the car, gave the friendliest smile he could muster and greeted them with a bright 'Good afternoon, ladies!'

No one knew quite how old the Currie twins were, but no one could actually remember them ever having been young. Neither could anyone recall them ever having done anything more adventurous or spontaneous than perhaps once leaving their cottage without wearing coats when June had scarcely begun.

'"Good" is a matter of opinion,' said Nessie, who always spoke first.

'Matter of opinion,' said Jessie, who had a curious compulsion always to repeat the very last words her sister uttered.

'And why would this beautiful sunny afternoon not be a good one?' Hamish asked, giving them, and Davey, a bewildered look. 'Has something upset you both?'

'Something certainly has,' Nessie said, taking a quick breath to move on before her sister could interrupt. 'You will no doubt have noticed that we're walking on the road.'

'On the road,' chorused Jessie, seizing her chance.

'Aye, I've noticed that, right enough,' Hamish agreed.

'Can you imagine why we're walking on the road?' Nessie asked.

'On the road,' Jessie repeated.

'Well, I'd guess it's because it's no' so slippery underfoot – we had the snow plough come in and clear the snow off the road.'

'So you say,' Nessie said with a curt nod, 'and where did the snow go that was on the road?'

'On the road,' Jessie chimed in again.

'Ah, now I see,' Hamish said, removing his cap and

running a hand through his hair, hoping it would give the impression that he was properly considering their problem. 'The snow's been pushed onto the pavement, so you're having to walk on the road.'

'Exactly!' said Nessie, sounding relieved that Hamish was finally beginning to understand. 'It also pushed the snow across our front gate. We had to climb out over a pile near as high as Ben Nevis! I slipped and bruised my coccyx on the road.'

'On the road,' said Jessie, sounding a little disappointed at the lack of variety Nessie was affording her.

'I'm sorry to hear that,' Hamish said. 'We've a couple of shovels in the back of the car. We'll stop by your house now and dig a path through the snow for you.'

'Thank you,' Nessie said, with what sounded like genuine gratitude. 'Perhaps you're not as useless and lazy as everyone says. You shall go to the top of my list of most helpful folk. Normally when I draw my list up, you're bottom.'

'Up your bottom!' chanted Jessie, delighted to have something different to say. Then she realised exactly what she *had* just said and her mouth fell open with shock. She looked at her sister, who scowled at her before they marched off in unison in the direction of the Patels' general-store-cum-post office. Hamish and Davey waited until they were safely back in the car before they both burst out laughing.

'A wee bit of snow clearing will be good exercise,' Davey said, 'and good for community relations.'

'It's no' just that,' Hamish said. 'The Currie twins can be right annoying, but it ay pays to keep in wi' them. They've helped me out many times in the past. They never miss a thing that goes on in Lochdubh.'

*

Later that day, Hamish walked along the shore road arm-in-arm with Claire, both of them well wrapped up against the cold. Although it was not yet six in the evening, it had already been dark for half an hour and the streetlights brought a twinkle to the frost coating the snow, even where the road muck had muddied the pristine white.

When Hamish pushed open the door of the Piper pub, they were immediately hit by a welcoming wall of warmth and began pulling off gloves and loosening their coats on the way to the bar. The landlord, Hector MacCrimmon, gave them a hearty greeting before pouring a glass of white wine for Claire and a pint of pale ale for Hamish. The pub walls were decorated with photographs of Hector, once a heavyweight boxer, either in the ring or posing with celebrities who barely came up to his shoulder, but it was the bagpipes displayed in a case behind the bar that caught Claire's eye.

'Will you be playing your pipes at the big wedding on Saturday, Hector?' she asked.

'Aye, they've asked me to be outside the kirk when the bride arrives and when the married couple come out,' Hector replied, 'then at the hotel to pipe as they arrive. I'll also be piping them into the dining room once all the guests have been seated.'

He cast an irritated glance across the room to where a few garbled words followed by hoots of laughter rang out. Seated at one of the many tables scattered around the pub were Darius Palmerston and Sebastian Chalmers, laughing loud enough to draw scowls from the locals sitting at the other tables.

'Mind you,' Hector went on, 'that's assuming yon bampot ower there actually makes it to his own wedding. He's no' been making himself too popular wi' my regulars. Him and his best man are the last o' the bunch that came in earlier and if they carry on causing a stramash as they have been, I've a mind to sling them oot.'

'It's your pub, Hector,' Hamish said, taking a sip of his pint. 'You decide who's welcome and who's no', but if you need me to have a word . . .'

'Thanks, Hamish,' Hector nodded, 'but I can handle the likes o' him.'

'As you will,' Hamish replied, 'but it would be a shame if he had to take his vows in the kirk wi' a black eye and a fat lip.'

Claire and Hamish took seats at a free table and were congratulating themselves on finally managing to arrange a night out together when Palmerston's voice drowned out all conversation.

'Did you hear about the deranged old headcase at the hotel this morning, Seb?' Palmerston said, almost choking on a swig of whisky. 'He was dancing around like a total blimp in the car park chanting a load of mumbo-jumbo!'

'Sloane said it was something about Jenny Horne – a witch who used to live there,' Chalmers said, laughing.

'Wouldn't surprise me,' Palmerston went on at full volume. 'Witches? What a load of absolute bollocks! Mind you, has anyone ever actually seen Priscilla's mother? It could be her! Maybe she's the witch!'

'You'd do well to mind your tongue, laddie,' an older man sitting at an adjacent table grumbled, pointing a finger at Palmerston. 'Talk like that's liable to upset folk in Lochdubh.'

'Ah, yes, I was told you were a superstitious lot up here,' Palmerston scoffed, 'but *witches*? Give me a break!'

'You need to show some respect for our history,' the man told him. 'The last person in Britain to be tried and executed for witchcraft was Janet Horne, no' far from here in Dornoch. There's a stone in the town marks the place where she was burnt alive.'

'Janet Horne?' Palmerston said with a sneer. 'Are you saying she was related to the hotel's Jenny?'

'Witches were ay known as Janet or Jenny Horne,' the old man explained.

'Is that so? And when was this?' Palmerston demanded.

'Seventeen twenty-seven,' came the response.

'So recent? Seventeen twenty-seven's just before half past five, isn't it – and it's barely gone six now!' Palmerston roared with laughter at his own joke, and Chalmers joined in for good measure.

'Are you mocking me, laddie?' growled the older man.

'Well of course I'm mocking you!' Palmerston snorted. 'You people need to grow up and start living in the twenty-first century! We were delayed by another couple of you numbskulls on our way up here today, weren't we, Seb? Seems the road wasn't wide enough for the idiots and they launched their car into a field.'

'You watch your mouth, pal,' a younger local snapped. 'That was my auntie and uncle crashed off the Strathbane road.'

'Oh, here we go!' Palmerston grinned. 'I should have known there would be a relative in the bar. You heathens are all related, aren't you? Proper inbreds, I hear. Let's have a look at your hands. What – only five fingers on each? I'd have expected at least six!'

The young man jumped to his feet, about to launch

himself at Palmerston when Hector's mighty paw landed on his shoulder, pushing him back into his seat. The big landlord then stepped towards Palmerston, towering over him.

'I think it's time you left,' he said.

'Ah, the prizefighter from the photographs!' Palmerston said, seemingly unfazed. 'Are you threatening me, old man?'

'No, he's being polite,' Hamish said, standing at Hector's side and holding his police warrant card in Palmerston's face. 'I'm threatening you. Leave now or you'll be spending the night in my police cell, and the bed's no' near as comfy as any in Tommel Castle.'

'Come on, Seb,' Palmerston said, tutting and rolling his eyes. 'If we go now, we'll still have time to change for dinner.'

With that, the bridegroom and his best man drained their glasses, grabbed their coats from the backs of their chairs and headed for the door. Following a brief round of muttering about the 'bloody English', conversation among the pub's regulars returned to more important, perennial matters such as Scottish football, Scottish independence, whether a Scotch pie should be eaten with ketchup or brown sauce and why, if global warming is real, they were up to their knees in snow.

Hamish and Claire were chatting about what they might do the next time they could catch some proper time off together. Their working shift patterns sometimes made spending time with each other difficult to arrange.

'Now that Davey's properly settled in as my constable,' Hamish said, 'I think we can be a wee bit more flexible about things. Maybe you and I can get away for a bit.'

'Hamish Macbeth!' Claire held her hand to her chest as though astounded. 'Did I just hear you say you wanted to "get away" from Lochdubh?'

'Aye, well, maybe no' get away as such . . .' Hamish began, then paused when she burst out laughing.

'I'm only pulling your leg, Hamish,' she said, pushing her blonde hair back from her face. 'I ken fine how much you love it here.'

'Well, I do,' he agreed, 'and there's an awfy lot I want to share wi' you. Even though you've lived here all your life, I bet you've never been to the Wailing Widow falls north o' Loch Assynt, or the falls at Loch Glencoul. They're the highest in the land and . . .'

Claire looked up and frowned as Elspeth walked into the bar.

'Hamish,' she said out of the corner of her mouth, 'tell me you didn't invite your ex-fiancée to join us tonight.'

'No' really . . .' Hamish said carefully. 'Elspeth just wants to have a wee word.'

Elspeth hurried over to their table.

'I can't stay long,' she said, 'but I've got to talk to you about that wedding party, Hamish. I've got a really bad feeling about the whole wedding and some of the people there really aren't what they seem.'

'Do tell,' Claire said, suddenly interested.

'What is it that's bothering you, Elspeth?' Hamish asked.

'Well, when my boss asked me to come up here to cover the wedding, I decided to do some research on the family,' Elspeth explained. 'Top of the tree is Charles Hamilton. His company has offices in London and Glasgow and he owns homes in the north and the south. His wife, Pamela – Alannah's mother – was widely reported to have died of cancer about ten years ago.

'The thing is, I've talked to staff who worked at Hamilton's properties and more than one has said that Pamela Hamilton didn't die of cancer at all.'

'So what happened to her?' asked Claire.

'My sources say she was an addict,' Elspeth said, gravely. 'She was hooked on painkillers but also cannabis, eventually heroin as well. Instead of getting her the help she needed, Hamilton hid her away. He kept her out of sight at the house near Glasgow to avoid any kind of scandal that might reflect badly on his business.'

'If he could do that,' Hamish said, 'surely he could have brought in professionals to care for her and wean her off the drugs.'

'He tried that for a while,' said Elspeth, 'but Pamela was very good at escaping and heading into the seediest parts of town looking for a fix. That made her a scandal just waiting to explode. In the end, he kept her locked away and stopped her from even trying to escape by supplying her with whatever drugs she craved. In the meantime, he'd been seeing someone else in London and set her up in an apartment in Mayfair – Serena. She was a dancer, a showgirl, and they were married when Pamela died of "cancer", although I now believe the cause of death was actually an overdose.'

'Are you saying that Hamilton killed his first wife?' Hamish asked.

'I think it's highly likely,' Elspeth said, 'but I've no real proof.'

'That's no' such an easy thing to get away wi', is it, Hamish?' Claire asked.

'No' easy, but no' impossible,' Hamish replied. 'If you've enough money to line the pockets o' doctors and the like, it could be done.'

'He certainly has the money,' Elspeth confirmed, 'and money appears to be at the heart of a family upset on the groom's side, from what I gather. Darius Palmerston seems to be a complete outcast when it comes to his own family.'

'This is better than one o' yon TV soaps!' Claire said, laughing. 'What's up wi' the Palmerstons then, Elspeth?'

'All I've been able to find out,' Elspeth continued, 'is that Darius's mother and father died in a car crash twelve years ago. They left a substantial amount of money but before the family could even figure out if there was a will, Darius disappeared along with his friend Sebastian and all of the money.'

'The pair o' them joined the army, did they no'?' Hamish said.

'I haven't yet found any military records for either of them,' said Elspeth, 'but I've got people looking into that. The only relatives of his parents I could find didn't want to talk to me. No one's seen either Darius or Sebastian since they supposedly went off to join the army.'

'No one?' Claire asked, surprised. 'What about Sebastian's parents?'

'His mother is dead and his father has disowned him,' Elspeth explained. 'For some reason, his family don't want to know him. The Hamiltons insisted that invitations went out to Palmerston's family, but only two cousins responded – Stephen Palmerston and Henry Poulter – and those two young men have never actually met him. They've come along just for fun.'

'If Darius and his best man fell out wi' their families and joined the army to get away from them all,' Hamish reasoned, 'it helps to explain why the wedding is taking place here in Lochdubh, hundreds of miles from their kin.'

'But it's still very odd,' Elspeth said, 'and I have a dreadful feeling every time I come near Darius or Sebastian. They're hiding something, and it's all going to come to a head at the wedding the day after tomorrow.'

'Well, I can't say I ever knew a wedding that went entirely smoothly,' Claire said, smiling and clearly finding the whole saga hugely entertaining, 'but maybe this will all sort itself out when the happy couple finally tie the knot.'

'I very much doubt that,' Elspeth said. 'I can guarantee you there will be no happy ending to this story.'

Chapter Three

*He has no notion of the solemnity of marriage . . .
or he would look less jolly. I would not like a man
that joked about his marriage.*
                J. M. Barrie, 'Life in a Country Manse –
                          A Wedding in a Smiddy' (1892)

Elspeth rose to leave and there were murmurs of recognition from the locals sitting nearby, one old man asking his two friends in a foghorn voice that he thought was a whisper, 'Is that no' yon lassie off the telly?' Since leaving Sutherland, Elspeth had made regular appearances on the screen in everyone's living rooms presenting the TV news and those she had left behind were proud that one of their own had become such a celebrity. She smiled and nodded greetings to anyone looking in her direction, then turned back to Hamish and Claire.

'I have to get back,' she said. 'I'm a one-woman camera team on this job and I need to film a few short interviews. If I find out any more about the wedding party, I'll let you know.'

'That's fine by me,' Hamish replied, 'although, as far as I can tell, there's nothing I need to get involved in. No crime's been committed.'

'Charles Hamilton may have murdered his first wife,' Claire pointed out.

'Aye, but we've no proof o' that,' Hamish said. 'Still, it seems that there's more to these folk than meets the eye. I'm on one o' my rest days in the morn, so I'm taking some o' them out on a hike in the snow. Maybe I'll find out a wee bit more about them then.'

'Where are you taking them?' Claire asked.

'Ben Diabhail and the Spaniard's Leap,' he answered.

'Be careful, Hamish,' Claire said. 'It's dangerous out in the hills wi' snow on the ground.'

'It's an easy walk,' Hamish said, 'and I'll keep them all well back from the edge o' the Leap. A snow cornice builds up there and it's never stable enough to stand on.'

'I'll see you at the hotel in the morning, then,' Elspeth said. 'Maybe I can grab some shots of the walkers heading off into the snow. Sorry for butting in on your pre-Valentine evening.'

'No worries,' Claire said. 'On Saturday – Valentine's night – Hamish is taking me to sample the seafood up at the Kylesku Hotel. It's where we went on our very first date.'

'Hamish Macbeth, you old romantic!' Elspeth said, then she and Claire laughed as Hamish's face flushed crimson.

The guests who had chosen to participate in the two outings gathered in the bar area for coffee at 8 a.m., shortly after sunrise. Darius, Sebastian, Viscount Carsely and Simon Derringer, along with Darius's cousins Stephen Palmerston and Henry Poulter, had decided to go on the fishing trip. Alannah and her bridesmaids, Sloane

Beaumont and Helen Carter, were to be joined by a handful of other female guests on the mountain walk. Priscilla was there to greet everyone and, once they'd all seated themselves, she reassured those who had not yet had breakfast that they still had time should they wish to do so.

'We want both the fishing party and the walkers to be out by nine in order to make the most of the daylight hours,' she said. 'We're expecting fair weather and clear skies today but, to be on the safe side, we need everyone to be back early in the afternoon, long before we start to lose the light.

'For those of you going fishing, the cars will take you down to the harbour where Mr Maclean will meet you. My father is joining you, so will be on hand should you have any questions while you're out.

'For everyone going hillwalking, we're very lucky to have a hugely experienced local guide – Lochdubh's Police Sergeant Hamish Macbeth.'

There was a spontaneous burst of applause and Hamish, slightly taken aback by the enthusiasm of his welcome, stepped forward to stand beside a whiteboard over which was draped a large map of the area.

'Good grief!' came Darius's whining tone. 'It's the one from the pub, Seb. I'm glad I'm going fishing.'

'Good morning to you, too, Mr Palmerston,' Hamish said, smiling directly at him, 'and can I just say that I'm also glad you're going fishing.'

'Time I had some breakfast,' Darius snorted. He got up and stalked off to the dining room, followed by Sebastian. Hamish turned to the map and traced their route with an outstretched hand.

'Today we're going to head up towards Ben Diabhail

and take a path that runs across this northern slope. We'll follow it round to where the River Anstey cascades down a gorge here at a place called "The Spaniard's Leap" where there are some grand views to take in. Looking inland, we should be able to see as far as Ben More Assynt and beyond, and I'll be able to point out mountains like Beinn Dearg to the south. To the west, we can look out across the North Minch to see the hills on the Isle of Lewis, so there will be lots of photo opportunities for you.'

'What was that mountain you mentioned?' Sloane Beaumont asked. 'The first one – the one we'll be going up. What does the name mean?'

'Ben Diabhail,' Hamish said. 'It means Devil's Mountain.'

'I thought it sounded a bit like "Devil",' she said. 'Would that be the Devil who got married here?'

'So legend would have it,' Hamish confirmed, 'but I doubt we'll be meeting him today. Hopefully, we'll see an eagle or two and, when we come down off the top, mountain hare and deer on the lower slopes.'

'And what was that you said about the Spaniard's leap?' Sloane asked. 'He must have leapt a long way if he landed here in Scotland!'

There were a few laughs and Hamish joined in with a good-natured grin.

'Actually, miss, there were quite a few Spaniards landed here, but they didn't jump,' he explained. 'When the king o' Spain sent an armada to invade England in 1588, the English fought them off down south and then chased them all the way up their east coast as far as Scotland.

'We weren't exactly best o' pals wi' the English at the time, so the Spanish ships were welcome when some put in to Scottish ports for repairs and supplies. They then planned a route that would take them all the way round the north o' Scotland from where they could avoid the English navy and head south back to Spain. Sadly, several ships were wrecked in storms off the west coast here and in Ireland. Some o' the Spanish who made it to land chose to settle in Scotland and were made welcome, but there was one who came into Loch Dubh in a small boat who seemed a bit strange. He was alone and came ashore wi' a large sea chest.

'Rumours soon spread that he was carrying a fortune in gold coins. There were ay rumours about Spanish treasure on the wrecked ships – gold and silver brought to pay their troops. The rumours attracted all the worst kind o' cutthroats, seeking out the Spaniard and his gold. The Spaniard fled from the cottage where he'd been given shelter but then, as now, the only way out o' the village was across the bridge.

'He knew he'd be caught if he took that route, so he began climbing into the hills, taking the same path we'll be walking today. By the time he reached the Anstey gorge, he realised that he had to cross the river to escape, and by now he could see the villains back on the path further down the mountain, closing in on him. At the narrowest part o' the gorge, he decided he could jump from the wide ledge where he was standing to the slightly lower cliff top on the far side.'

Hamish paused to take a sip of coffee and Sloane piped up again.

'Well, come on, Sergeant Hamish,' she gushed, treating him to what she considered her most alluring smile. 'Don't leave us in suspense! We want to know what happened to our poor Spaniard.'

'Wi' his pursuers hot on his heels, the Spaniard took a run at the gap and hurled himself towards the other side wi' all his might,' Hamish went on. 'Those chasing him saw him flying through the air, knowing he'd get clean away once on the other side. None o' them would have been brave enough to follow. But the Spaniard had reckoned without the weight o' the gold he had stuffed in every pocket and he didn't quite make it. He tumbled down into the gorge and was swept away by the river. His body was never recovered and neither was any o' his precious treasure, although many have gone searching for it ower the years. To my knowledge, no one since has ever tried to clear the Spaniard's Leap.'

'And what about you, Sergeant Hamish?' Sloane said, raising an eyebrow suggestively. 'You're tall and strong. Do you think you could manage it?'

There were a few giggles from the ladies present and Hamish began to blush again, just as he'd done with Elspeth and Claire the night before.

'Well, he is a bit of an athlete, actually, aren't you, Sergeant Hamish?' Priscilla said, with an impish smile, using the name Sloane had conjured up to join in the teasing. 'Three times outright winner of the mountain run at the Strathbane Games.'

'Ooh, I find that so attractive in a man—' Sloane began before Alannah cut her off, laughing.

'Stop flirting with the sergeant, Sloane!' she said, giving her friend a playful shove.

'I'm told you all have good hillwalking clothes and jackets,' Hamish said. 'You'll be able to walk the path in decent hiking boots. Priscilla has a selection of snow gaiters if you don't have your own. Finally, when it comes to clothes, no jeans, please.'

'Why not jeans?' Darius was now standing in the door to the dining room munching on a huge breakfast bap stuffed with sausage and bacon.

'I'd have thought you'd know that as a former army man,' Hamish replied. 'If denim gets wet, it stays wet and will chill you to the bone. It's no' the thing for a mountain walk.'

'If you say so,' Darius said with a shrug, taking another bite of his bap.

'Come on everyone,' Alannah said, standing. 'In you go for breakfast before Darius scoffs the lot!'

'Seems like the chief bridesmaid has taken a bit of a fancy to you, Hamish,' Silas said, joining Hamish by the whiteboard.

'Aye, well . . .' Hamish replied, still a little embarrassed by the unwanted attention, 'I can do without all that on our wee hike. I'm glad I'll have you along, though, Silas. Will you bring up the rear and watch out for stragglers?'

'I don't think you'll have a problem with stragglers, Sergeant,' said Alannah. 'We're all outdoorsy types and used to long hikes.'

She had brought Paul Hunter, the groom, to introduce him to Hamish and slipped her arm through Paul's, giving it a squeeze as she did so.

'This is Paul, Sergeant Macbeth,' she said. 'He's an absolute treasure. He looks after our horses and he's going to join us on our walk.'

'Pleased to meet you, Paul,' Hamish said, shaking hands. 'So you think they'll all cope wi' our wee mountain trip?'

'I know most of those coming on the hike,' Paul said. 'They're all fairly fit and perfectly capable. More so than me, I should think – I hope I don't become one of your stragglers!' He gave a quick laugh. 'Even with me tagging along, though, it should be plain sailing.'

'I'm sure you're right,' Hamish said, watching Darius and Sebastian leaving the dining room. Darius picked up an apple from a fruit bowl on the way out. 'Somehow I think it's the fishing trip that's no' going to be such plain sailing.'

With the two excursion parties divided roughly into male and female guests, Darius declared the fishing trip a 'stag do'. None of the women showed any interest in fishing barring Sloane who, despite the fact that she was actually going on the mountain walk, suggested that Sebastian could show her how to handle his rod. Elspeth filmed the fishing group embarking in the cars in the sunshine and the walkers trudging off into the snow like an arctic expedition. Charles Hamilton and his wife, along with Robert Jensen and most of the other wedding guests, chose to spend the day relaxing in the hotel.

When the cars reached the harbour, Archie Maclean was standing at the quayside, waiting by his boat, *Bluebell*, with a burly young man. He introduced his companion as his nephew, Donald.

'We meet again, Donald,' Darius said, recognising the young man from the Piper the previous evening. 'I hope the old man can steer his boat better than your other uncle can drive his car!'

Donald scowled at him, then shinned down a short ladder onto the boat to help the others board. He left Palmerston to manage on his own.

Bluebell was barely twenty feet in length but had a surprisingly spacious deck with a wheelhouse and small cabin up front and two hatches, one above the engine and the other above the hold. The fishing party seated themselves on the hatches while Donald handed out life-jackets and Archie started the engine. The marine diesel clattered into life, then settled into a constant rhythm that coursed through *Bluebell*'s wooden planks and hull. Moments later they were heading out onto the loch, causing ripples that made the white reflections of the Twin Sisters mountains shimmer on the surface. Darius bit into the apple he had brought with him, then paused as a seal popped its head above the surface near the boat. He hurled his apple at the seal, inevitably missing the wily creature.

'Bugger off!' he yelled at the seal. 'We don't want you pinching our fish!'

'Cut that out!' Donald said, stepping between Darius and the side of the boat.

'Why, what's it to you?' Darius sneered. 'Was that another of your relatives?'

'Donald!' Archie called, and pointed to the wheel. Donald glowered at Darius then swapped places with his uncle.

Archie wasn't a big man, but he stood squarely in front of Darius, the grizzled stubble on his chin complementing his grim expression. The look wasn't unusual for Archie. The truth was, he rarely smiled, preserving the few teeth he had left in his mouth for eating rather than greeting. Nevertheless, he always managed to snare people's attention with the ever-present, thinly rolled cigarette clamped in the corner of his mouth. Whether lit or not, the slim white appendage bobbed around like a conductor's baton, directing the sonata of his wisdom.

'You'd do well to respect our ways while you're on my boat, laddie,' he said. 'Yon seal is entitled to his share o' the fish in the loch. The water is his world, after all, no' ours. Some say seals are the souls o' seafarers lost to the waves, so we don't grudge them a bit o' whatever we might catch. If, on the other hand, he's a selkie, then best leave him well alone.'

'A what?' Darius scoffed. 'What the hell is a selkie? Some weird new seal species?'

'No' a new species,' Donald advised him from the wheelhouse. 'Selkies have existed as long as anyone can remember. They take the form o' a seal but they can shed their sealskins at the water's edge and walk the earth as a human. Harm a selkie and they'll take their revenge.'

'More superstitious crap!' Darius laughed at Donald. 'Honestly – coming up here's like time travel. It's like we're back in the Middle Ages!'

Donald stared at Darius with undisguised contempt, then turned back to the wheel.

'Come along now, gentlemen,' the colonel piped up, keen to lighten the atmosphere. 'We have flasks of coffee to warm you while we head out to the best fishing spots.' He then produced a bottle of Glenmorangie from an inside pocket. 'We also have a wee dram for the coffee to steady your sea legs!'

The two excursions were a huge success, the fishermen boastfully proud of their catches and the walkers utterly delighted to have seen a pair of eagles soaring above the slopes of Ben Diabhail. That evening after dinner, the bridegroom, and as many of his entourage who could be persuaded to brave the cold, headed down to the Piper for what Darius described as 'a booze-up to commemorate my last night of freedom'.

Archie Maclean and Donald were also on their way to the pub, the old man having promised his nephew a couple of pints on top of his wage as a reward for his hard work that day. They were chatting as they walked along the shore road but paused, stepping into a shadow when they spotted Darius and his crowd ahead of them.

'I'm sorry, Uncle Archie,' Donald said, 'but I can't go into the Piper if he's going to be there. If he starts winding me up just one more time, I'm liable to kill the bastard!'

'Come away, Donald,' Archie said, taking his nephew's arm and leading him back the way they had come, 'and let's have no more o' that talk. We'll pay the Piper a visit another night, but don't you go doing your dinger ower the likes o' Darius Palmerston. In a couple o' days, he'll be gone from our lives for ever. In the meantime, there's good money to be made out o' those folk. You're working at the hotel the morn, are you no'?'

'Aye, but maybe I should call off. The thought o' serving at yon scunner's wedding fair turns my stomach.'

'Nonsense, laddie,' Archie said, sternly. 'You don't want to let the hotel down. There'll be more work for you there in future. You just keep your heid and take the money.'

'You're right,' Donald said, with a heavy sigh. 'Let's away home.'

In the cottage beside which they were standing, the curtains twitched in an upstairs window as the two men strolled off into the night.

*

Sloane Beaumont collapsed onto her single bed, creaking the springs and drawing a sleepy mumble from her roommate and fellow bridesmaid, Helen Carter, in the adjacent bed.

'I thought you were coming up ages ago,' Helen complained. 'Alannah warned us not to stay up too late tonight. We need our beauty sleep.'

'Speak for yourself!' Sloane said, laughing. 'I decided to wait up until the boys got back from the pub. I wanted to see Seb. He's quite cute, don't you think?'

'I suppose so,' Helen said, yawning.

'Well, we chatted for ages. I thought we were getting on like a house on fire and then I walked upstairs with him,' Sloane said, lowering her voice to a level of breathless confidentiality. 'I managed to corner him in the second-floor corridor and put my arms round his neck. I went to kiss him – but he turned away! I mean – what's wrong with the men in this place? I thought the best man and the ushers were supposed to go all out to bag a bridesmaid and I couldn't even get a quick snog outside the broom cupboard!'

'Maybe you're just not his type,' Helen offered, snuggling back down beneath her duvet.

'That's not the point,' argued Sloane. 'Give a guy enough to drink and he completely forgets whatever "his type" is . . . or does he? Maybe that's something I'll talk to him about tomorrow.'

'You do that,' Helen said. 'Now hurry up and put out the light. I need to get back to sleep!'

Hamish stood in the garden behind his police station, sipping his first mug of coffee of the morning and gazing out over Loch Dubh. Gone were the perfect reflections of the mountains, the images now distorted by breeze-blown waves on the incoming tide. The weather was changing. He was sure it felt a degree or two warmer than the previous morning, and a scattering of clouds was drifting in off the sea.

'Snow before nightfall, Lugs,' he said, reaching down to ruffle the fur on his dog's head. Sitting in front of Lugs, Sonsie, his huge pet cat, looked up at him with hooded yellow eyes. It was an open secret among the locals that Sonsie wasn't just a big tabby – she was a Scottish wildcat. While it was strictly forbidden for anyone to keep one of these rare and supposedly untameable animals, no one would ever contemplate reporting their local police sergeant. This was less out of loyalty to Hamish than it was out of fear that he and Sonsie should ever be parted. He'd been like a bear with a hangover when he'd once released her into the wild at the sanctuary down at Ardnamurchan. The whole village had breathed a collective sigh of relief when he decided he missed her so much that he went back to find her and bring her home.

The cat blinked and nodded, apparently agreeing with his weather forecast, then returned to her meticulous grooming regime.

'Post's in, Hamish!' Davey called, chirpily, stepping out of the kitchen door with a slice of buttered toast in one hand and two large, pink envelopes in the other. 'Look – one for each of us!'

'One what?' Hamish asked, then his face fell when he realised what Davey was carrying. 'Crivens! It's Valentine's Day!'

'Aye, course it is,' Davey agreed. 'You didn't forget, did you?'

'No' really ...' Hamish said with a groan, 'but ... well ... are we no' a bit auld for all that malarkey?'

'You'd best not let Claire hear you saying that!' Davey laughed. 'Especially when there's romance in the air with this big wedding today. If you want a quiet life, you need to get down to the Patels' shop and pick up a card – flowers, too, given you've left it so late that you'll have to present the card in person.'

'I thought that having a fancy dinner would be enough and—' Hamish began, but he gave up when Davey sighed and shook his head.

'Hamish,' he said, 'you really ought to know better than that.'

Hamish took his envelope indoors and opened it in his office. Inside was a colourful yet tastefully designed card from Claire, proclaiming how much she loved him. He stood it on his desk and hurried off to the shop, where he was appalled by the scant selection of fewer than a dozen cards on the rack. They were all either so slushy and sentimental that he could barely finish reading the saccharine verses inside, or they were so vulgar as to be practically obscene.

'No' much left on the rack today, Hamish,' Mrs Patel consoled him once he had found what he considered the least offensive card. 'All the good ones went ower the last couple o' days.'

'Aye, I can tell,' Hamish said. 'Have you any fresh flowers, Mrs Patel?'

'We had some bonny roses,' she replied, 'but they're all gone, too.'

Hamish paid for the card and rushed back to the station, setting off almost immediately with Davey in response to a call that had come in about an abandoned car on the road to Scourie. By the time they had dealt with that and calmed a rowdy domestic dispute in Braikie, a few lazy flakes of snow were falling as they drove back into Lochdubh. The storm was enjoying a gentle overture to its performance.

The wedding was also underway and they pulled over to watch Darius, Sebastian and their ushers walk up the stone steps into the church. They were all wearing black 'Prince Charlie' jackets and kilts either in red-and-blue or darker green-and-blue versions of the Hamilton tartan. Hamish and Davey skirted a gaggle of locals who had gathered to watch the proceedings and approached Elspeth, who had filmed the groom and his party arriving.

'Yon outfits must have cost a pretty penny,' Hamish said, watching the kilted men making their way into the church.

'The kilts were provided courtesy of Charles Hamilton – he can afford it,' Elspeth said. 'All very glamorous, but we haven't seen the bride yet. She took breakfast in her room this morning so that her husband wouldn't see her on the morning of the wedding until they're in church. She'll be the star of the show and . . . what on earth is that?'

Elspeth pointed to where two vehicles were approaching slowly from the direction of the Anstey bridge. The first was a large and battered American saloon. It was black with a white roof and white front doors that each boasted a big gold star. It was followed by a grey van. Hamish stepped into the road to flag down the car. He looked inside to see two men in black suits with white shirts, black ties, black sunglasses and black fedora hats.

'Good morning, sir,' Hamish said when the driver wound down the window. 'What in the name o' the wee man is this?'

'Do you no' ken a Blues Mobile when you see one?' said the driver, laughing. 'We're the band ... for the wedding.'

'I have the feeling they were expecting a ceilidh band for the highland dancing,' Hamish said.

'Aye, we do a braw job wi' a ceilidh!' announced a long-haired young man who had just stepped out of the van. 'Is that no' right, Andy?'

He was joined by another man whereupon they launched into an impromptu rendition of 'Mairi's Wedding', linking arms to reel each other round in the snow. The driver asked for directions to Mrs Mackenzie's boarding house, where the band would be staying overnight.

'It's right up the end o' the street here,' Hamish said pointing into the distance, 'but maybe just hold on a wee minute. Here comes the bride.'

The drone of a bagpipe's bladder inflating filled the air, followed by the skirl of 'Highland Cathedral' as Hector MacCrimmon marched forward to play for the arrival of the bride. Blaze and Brandy trotted along the road, drawing a dark blue, open carriage through a light dusting of settling snow. The carriage's coachwork was highlighted with flourishes of gold and Paul sat at the high driver's seat, holding the horses' reins. He was smartly dressed in a black jacket and bowler hat with light grey breeches and a waistcoat. Seated in the carriage were Alannah and her father, accompanied by the two bridesmaids, Sloane and Helen. Paul drew the carriage to a halt outside the church and there was a cheer from the crowd. He jumped down to open the carriage door for Charles Hamilton, whose kilt outfit somehow managed to look a little more splendid than the others in the wedding party. Paul placed a stepping block on the ground for him to disembark, both men then offering their hands to support Alannah.

Her dress was a figure-hugging symphony of silk and lace with long lace sleeves and a sweeping train which Sloane and Helen stood ready to hold. She wore a white fox-fur shawl over her shoulders and a white veil, held in place by a diamond tiara. The veil drifted on a waft of breeze like a wisp of pale smoke when she took her father's and Paul's hands to step down onto the pavement. She smiled at the crowd, who were now applauding with gloved hands, snow crowning their woolly hats and spotting Charles Hamilton's black jacket like premature confetti.

'Yon's a right bonny bride,' said the driver of the Blues Mobile. 'Is that real fur and diamonds?'

'From what I hear o' the Hamilton family,' Hamish replied, 'only the real thing would be good enough.'

'I told you we'd no' charged them enough,' grumbled a voice from the passenger seat.

Hamish watched Elspeth, having filmed the bride's arrival, quickly skip up the steps to be ready to film inside the church. Hector changed his tune to Wagner's 'Bridal Chorus' when Alannah and her father reached the top of the steps, following them to the door of the church where he stood, filling the interior with music as the proud father walked his daughter up the aisle.

Paul stood beside the horses, watching the bridal party disappear into the church, hardly noticing when Davey strolled over to him.

'Blaze and Brandy and the carriage look fantastic,' Davey said, and Paul turned away from the church, fussing over Brandy's harness.

'Yes . . . yes they do,' he said. 'Thank you.'

'Are you not going inside?' Davey asked.

'No, my place is out here with the horses,' Paul replied, looking glum. 'I've blankets to throw over them to keep the snow off. I need to cover the carriage seats, as well. Everything's being run like clockwork and Alannah will be out with her new husband in precisely forty-five minutes. She'll be Mrs Palmerston then.'

'I'll leave you to it, Paul,' Davey said, perplexed by why the groom was looking so down in the mouth. He patted the horses before joining Hamish by his Land Rover.

'He's no' looking awfy happy,' Hamish said, nodding towards Paul.

'No,' Davey said, climbing into the car, 'and he and Alannah seem like the best of pals. You'd think he'd be pleased for her.'

Exactly forty-five minutes after Alannah Hamilton entered the church, she walked out as Alannah Palmerston on her husband's arm. Hector piped them out to 'The Highland Wedding' and confetti was thrown by guests and locals. Hector then hurried on by car ahead of the carriage, as did Elspeth, to be on hand for the married couple's arrival at the hotel.

The bride and groom paused in the hotel entrance to be photographed flanked by vases of red and white roses, the flowers tied with Hamilton tartan ribbons, before welcoming their guests into the wedding reception. As everyone filed in, Robert Jensen sought out Elspeth.

'How is it all going?' he asked, accepting a glass of champagne from a cruising waiter. 'Did you get everyone arriving at the church? Did you get Charles and Alannah walking up the aisle?'

'Aye, of course, Robert,' Elspeth assured her boss, 'but, you know, any wedding photographer could have done that.'

'But no photographer or videographer would conduct interviews like you can,' he countered.

'That may be so,' Elspeth said, 'but I'm going to end up with enough footage for an entire documentary, not just a few seconds on the evening news.'

'Good,' he said, smiling. 'That's just what I want. I want you to edit it all together as a documentary, and that will be my wedding present to the happy couple. Film everything – I don't want you to miss a thing. Just keep your camera rolling. It's digital, after all, so you can record hours of stuff without any problem.'

Although not entirely happy about being seconded onto her boss's private project that had little or nothing to do with her usual diet of news and current affairs, Elspeth dutifully did as she was told, filming, interviewing guests and staff, and leaving her camera sitting on a tripod recording whatever came to pass whenever she took a break or paused for a glass of champagne.

Silas stood in the doorway of a small sitting room that led off from the bar. The door was closed behind him and he looked out over the guests laughing and chatting. As the bride, Alannah was the centre of attention with everyone anxious to offer their congratulations. Her bridesmaids, Sloane and Helen, were ever attentive but Silas wondered for a moment where Darius was. He wasn't with Sebastian, who was standing with the viscount, Simon Derringer and Alannah's father. Then Silas spotted Darius coming into the bar from the dining room with Serena Hamilton, just as he had done the previous day.

Something then happened that Silas couldn't quite believe. Just before they joined the main body of guests, Darius casually reached behind Serena and gently tweaked her left buttock. Silas braced himself for a screech of outrage and winced when he imagined the furious smack in the face he expected Serena to inflict upon Darius. Yet there was no drama and barely any reaction at all. Serena simply looked at Darius, smiled, gave him a sly wink and mouthed the words, 'Not here.' *That*, pondered Silas, *is not the way a freshly married husband and his stepmother-in-law should be behaving.*

The colonel then appeared, approached Darius and offered a firm handshake, Serena drifting off through the crowd towards her husband.

'Congratulations, my boy,' the colonel said, holding a modest glass of whisky in his free hand and raising it in a hint of a toast. 'I wish you and your lovely bride every happiness.'

'Thank you, sir,' Darius replied, patently aware that a man everyone referred to as 'the colonel' had, at one time, held a significant military rank. He raised his glass to acknowledge the gesture from the colonel.

'I hear you were an army man, as was I,' the colonel said. 'Who were you with?'

'Household Cavalry,' Darius responded. 'Chocolate-box soldiers, some called us, but the cavalry mixes it with the enemy just like any other regiment – tanks, not horses, of course.'

'Did you see any action?' the colonel asked.

'Not really, sad to say,' Darius answered. 'Seb and I spent ten years with the regiment but we were too late for Iraq or Afghanistan. We spent most of our time trotting around at Trooping of the Colour or charging across

Salisbury Plain in a Chieftain tank. The latter was more fun, quite frankly.'

'I see,' the colonel said, thoughtfully.

'I'm afraid I'm needed in the small breakfast room now, Colonel,' Darius said. 'Alannah wants to have the cake-cutting ceremony in there now, before we go in to the main dining room for the meal, so that our guests can be served a piece of cake post dessert. I'll be needing this.'

He reached out to a side table and picked up a long sword, unsheathing it slightly from its scabbard to reveal a shining blade, then dropping it back into place with a heavy click.

'My old cavalry sword,' Darius explained. 'I carried it countless times on parade but this is the first time it's actually been called on to cut something. We're using it to cut our wedding cake.'

'Are you indeed?' the colonel remarked, smiling politely and nodding. 'Then you must carry on.'

Darius strode off to the breakfast room, where Priscilla was demanding everyone's attention and Alannah was waiting, the wedding photographer standing by with his cameras and Elspeth already shooting some video. The colonel scurried off towards the hotel reception, muttering to himself. He walked straight past Silas en route.

'Everything all right, Colonel?' Silas asked.

'Chieftain tank my arse!' growled the colonel, heading for the staircase that led to his private quarters.

The cake-cutting ceremony went without a hitch, the base tier into which Alannah and Darius gently plunged the sword immediately whisked off to the kitchen, leaving the remaining four tiers standing on the table alongside the sword. Both Elspeth and the official wedding photographer made sure they captured those images before Priscilla once again called for everyone's attention.

'Staff in the dining room will now direct you to your tables,' she explained. 'The bride and groom will then take the top table with their entourage. Our chef has prepared a truly sumptuous feast for you, after which there will be speeches and toasts. We will then finish with wedding cake and drinks before we'll ask you all to join the bride and groom for a short spell in the bar while this room is reconfigured for the ceilidh.'

Everything went exactly as Priscilla had intimated. Seated at a table along with other guests, Elspeth set her camera on a tripod while her meal was served, but it was proving something of an obstacle for the waiters and waitresses so she popped it through a nearby door into the bar area, retrieving it to capture the speeches. It was when the majority of the guests were settled with their wedding cake, mingling between tables and filling the room with conversation, loudly amplified by the wine and whisky that had flowed during the meal, that Elspeth noticed Alannah sitting entirely alone at the top table. Darius, her father, Serena, Helen, Sloane, Robert and Sebastian all appeared to have deserted her.

Elspeth watched Alannah chat briefly with those guests who ventured up to the table to congratulate her, tell her once again how wonderful she looked, or remark on the exceptional meal, but as the minutes ticked by she clearly grew more and more uncomfortable about having been left on her own. She looked left and right, by now frustrated and impatient, having gone from being the centre of everyone's attention to having been abandoned. She stood, craning her neck to see through into the bar.

Suddenly Elspeth felt an icy chill flood her whole body. The myriad lively conversations around her dulled into a muffled fog and she only had eyes for Alannah. She knew without a doubt that something appalling was about to happen and rose to her feet, fixing the young bride with her stare. Alannah looked back at her with a puzzled expression. Elspeth took a couple of steps towards the top table then stopped, unable to move, overcome with a paralysing feeling of utter dread. She stood in the middle of the floor, trembling slightly. Those closest to her stopped talking and looked towards her. Their silence spread throughout the room and some could even hear Elspeth whispering.

'No . . . please, no . . . no . . .'

Alannah frowned, shook her head and walked towards the breakfast room. Elspeth made to cross the room to stop her but before she had fought her way past the first clutch of guests, Alannah had disappeared through the door.

Then there was a scream that left everyone in the dining room bristling with shock and Alannah staggered back in. Her face was pale, her eyes were filled with terror and the front of her wedding dress was stained red with blood. She held her hands out, blood dripping from her fingers, then collapsed on the floor.

Chapter Four

Nothing in his life became him like the leaving it.
     William Shakespeare, *Macbeth* (c. 1606)

A succession of screams pierced the air in the dining room and several guests rushed forward to where Alannah lay on the floor, drenched in blood. Silas sprinted into the room with Priscilla hot on his heels.

'Stay back, please, everyone!' Silas ordered, kneeling beside Alannah, who was on her back, motionless. He stopped for a fraction of a second, taken aback by the sight of her blood-soaked wedding dress, then put his fingers on her neck, feeling for a pulse. The vital heartbeat was there and he heard her give a soft groan, moving her head slightly, although her eyes remained closed. He talked to her constantly, repeating her name as he gently swept his hand across the darkest areas of blood on her dress and examined her hands. He could find no wounds.

'She's not injured,' he said. 'This isn't her blood. Priscilla, send for Dr Brodie!'

Priscilla, however, didn't move. She stood near the top table rooted to the spot, unable to tear her eyes away from the figure of the beautiful bride lying on the floor, the exquisite, delicately intricate lace of her dress now stained a horrifying red.

'Priscilla!' Silas roared. 'Get Dr Brodie now!'

Priscilla shuddered, appeared to come to her senses, produced her mobile phone and turned away, tapping the phone's screen. Freddy then lurched into the room, bounding over to kneel beside Silas.

'Stay with her, Freddy,' Silas said. 'I can't find any wounds, but keep talking to her.'

'Aye, she's in shock,' Freddy said, the gangly former policeman folding himself small to let Alannah know he was there and holding her bloodied hand. 'Stay calm, Alannah. Everything's going to be all right, lass.'

'Fetch a blanket and a pillow,' Silas said, getting to his feet and pointing at one of the hotel staff. 'We'll not move her until the doctor gets here, but we have to keep her warm. What exactly happened here?' he added, looking to the guests.

'We heard a scream and she appeared from in there,' explained Simon Derringer, pointing to the door that led to the breakfast room. Bizarrely, Silas suddenly remembered that he hadn't yet looked up what an 'Honourable' was.

'I'd best take a look, then,' he said, mentally scolding himself for losing concentration. 'Everyone else stay right here.'

He walked through into the breakfast room and returned a few seconds later with his phone in his hand.

'Hamish,' he said urgently, 'we need you here right now. There's been a murder.'

Hamish arrived at the hotel within minutes, dashing up the steps to the entrance alongside Davey, with Dr Brodie just behind them. Silas directed them through to the dining room where Charles Hamilton was now kneeling beside his daughter, sitting on his heels, the pleats of his kilt splayed out on the floor. He had added his black jacket to the blanket covering his daughter to keep her warm and, below his waistcoat, his shirt had come untucked from the waist of his kilt. The image of elegance, grace and glamour when the proud father had arrived at the church with his beautiful daughter just a few hours earlier could not have been in greater contrast to the scene of trauma, disarray and indignity on the dining-room floor.

Dr Brodie went straight to Alannah, setting his medical bag down and listening as Silas described exactly what had happened. Hamish glanced around the room, taking everything in. The wedding guests were gathered in groups, some sitting at tables, some standing, all looking pale and shocked. Paul Hunter, wearing an old jumper and jeans he clearly used for tending to the horses, was standing closest to Alannah and her father, wringing his hands, tears in his eyes.

Freddy was now guarding the door to the breakfast room. Priscilla and Elspeth were sitting at the top table, Priscilla drinking a glass of red wine and Elspeth staring at the table. She looked up, as if she knew Hamish was watching, and he could see her grey eyes were misty with tears. He went over to her and crouched beside her, gently putting his hand on her arm.

'I knew what she would find,' Elspeth said in little more than a whisper. 'I saw what was in there.'

'I'm sure you did, lass,' he said. 'You sit tight here wi' Priscilla. I need to go and take a look in there myself now.'

Hamish and Davey made for the breakfast room and Freddy stood aside.

'It's no' a pretty sight,' he said, looking more than a little shaken.

'Murder never is, Freddy,' Hamish replied. 'Bide where you are, Davey. The fewer people we have tromping around in here the better. We don't want to contaminate the crime scene any more than it already has been.'

He stood in the doorway, surveying the room, then took one pace inside to give himself a better view of the victim. Lying on his back on the floor, in a dark pool of blood, his kilt awry and his ceremonial sword plunged deep into his chest, was the body of Darius Palmerston. There was a deep cut, presumably a sword slash, to his neck below his left ear and his face was splashed with blood. It would be for the pathologist to determine, but in Hamish's opinion, that wound alone would have been enough to end Palmerston's life. The sword in his chest made doubly sure the deed was done. The grisly tableau was made even more macabre by the body's apparently relaxed pose. His eyes were closed, his hands were by his sides and his legs were crossed. Hamish frowned. This didn't look like the body of a man who'd been fighting for his life.

Next to the body was the round cake table, draped in a white tablecloth. It stood resolutely upright, displaying the remaining four complete, white-iced cake tiers. Through the window behind it, there was still enough daylight to see the snow falling gently in the garden against a green backdrop of trees. It would have made a beautiful photograph for any wedding album save for the fact that the tablecloth and the tall cake were spattered with blood.

'The white tower . . .' Hamish muttered.

'The what?' Davey asked from the doorway.

'Never mind,' Hamish said grimly. 'It was a warning we had no hope o' understanding.'

He looked at the two other doors leading out of the breakfast room, both closed.

'Silas, where do those other two doors go?' he asked and Silas squeezed into the doorway alongside Davey.

'That one goes through to the kitchen corridor,' he explained, 'and that one leads out to the doors that open onto the east terrace and the backstairs. I've locked them both so no one can come into the room that way.'

'Good thinking,' Hamish said. 'Would you now please go round the hotel and lock all the other outside doors, Silas? We don't want anyone leaving or entering the building. That might help to make sure that everyone who was here when Palmerston was murdered is still here. Davey, take the Land Rover down to the bridge and block the road. I don't want any vehicles leaving Lochdubh without us knowing exactly who's in them. In any case, anyone who was in the hotel this afternoon, if they've already left the building, is not to leave the village.'

Unlike the dining room, which had polished floorboards, the breakfast room had a beige carpet and Hamish noted that the blood spreading out from the body had been disturbed closest to where he was standing. There was a trail leading into the dining room. Those marks, he presumed, would have been made by the bride when she discovered her husband's body. He sighed. *Murdered on his wedding day*, he thought to himself, *and his bonny young bride discovers the body. It was an absolute tragedy.*

Hamish strode back into the dining room to see Priscilla helping herself to more wine and pouring a glass for Elspeth. Robert Jensen stormed over to Elspeth.

'What do you think you're doing?' he hissed. 'There's been a murder right here under our noses! This is the scoop of the century! Why are you sitting there drinking wine? Why aren't you filming?'

Elspeth stood, flung her wine in his face and sat down again. Priscilla refilled her glass.

'You'll regret that!' Jensen blustered, mopping his face with a table napkin, then whipping out his phone. 'I'm phoning the office right now and—'

'No, you're no',' Hamish said, reaching out to take the phone from Jensen's hand. He then raised his voice to address the whole room. 'In fact, I'll need all o' your phones. I'm sure you've all been taking photos today, at the church and back here at the hotel, so your phones may contain vital evidence. Priscilla will collect them from you. Thank you for your cooperation and don't worry, we'll take good care o' them. You'll have them back afore long. Priscilla?'

She jumped at the second mention of her name, looking up at him with an expression of mild confusion.

'I've no' enough evidence bags wi' me for all the phones,' he said. 'I know you have transparent plastic food bags in the kitchen. If you could bag each phone individually along wi' a note o' whose it is, and whatever passcodes they use, that would be grand.'

Apparently glad to have something useful to do, Priscilla went off to the kitchen. Hamish produced his own phone and called headquarters in Strathbane to report the murder, while walking through to the bar area. He then phoned Claire to explain what was going on.

'I'm right sorry, Claire,' he said, explaining about the murder. 'I was really looking forward to taking you up to Kylesku but we'll have to call it off. I'm going to be needed here.'

'Are you okay?' Claire asked. 'The whole thing at the hotel sounds awful.'

'I'm fine,' Hamish replied. 'I'll call the restaurant and cancel. I'll make it up to you, I promise.'

'Aye, well, the way the snow's coming down, we'd probably no' have made it anyway,' Claire said. 'I'll bide here at my place tonight and maybe go out for a drink wi' a couple o' work pals.'

When he rang off, Hamish looked up from his phone to see Richard Wade standing at the bar.

'Sounds like all this has ruined a special evening for you,' said the viscount.

'It's one o' the downsides o' this job,' Hamish said.

'It's a pity for your constable, too,' Wade said. 'A young man like him must have had plans for tonight.'

'He'd have been on duty anyway,' Hamish explained with a wry smile. 'I bagged tonight off. Privileges o' rank.'

'Glenfiddich, please,' Wade said, the barman having appeared. 'Make it a double. Can I offer you a drink, Sergeant?'

'I'd love a dram,' Hamish said, 'but I'll be needing my wits about me as the day goes on.'

'Very wise,' Wade complimented him, then turned to the barman who was pouring his drink. 'Actually, just give me the bottle, please. In fact, make it two. I'm sure there are plenty sitting in the dining room who could use a stiff drink. Charge it to my room.'

'That's very decent o' you,' Hamish said. 'Two bottles o' yon twenty-one-year-old single malt will cost you a packet.'

The viscount simply shrugged.
'Privileges of wealth,' he said.

By the time a convoy of police cars arrived from Strathbane, Hamish and Silas had compiled lists of everyone who was present in the hotel at the time of the murder either as wedding guests or working as staff. The colonel had been agitating to talk to Hamish and he had finally given in just as Hamish's old friend, DCI Jimmy Anderson, walked into the hotel reception following closely behind Superintendent Daviot.

'Jings!' Hamish breathed. 'It's the big boss himself!'

'Peter!' the colonel greeted Daviot with a handshake, the two being well acquainted. 'Terrible business this, isn't it?'

'It certainly is, George,' Daviot replied, 'and we'll do our utmost to get the whole mess sorted out for you as swiftly as we possibly can.'

'Yes, I've every confidence in you, of course,' the colonel said, 'and I really would like to have a word with you about the victim, Darius Palmerston.'

'All in good time, George,' Daviot said, with a hint of a grimace. To Hamish, he also looked a little pale. 'I'd like to freshen up a little after that long car journey.'

Daviot brushed past the colonel and walked briskly down the corridor to the gentlemen's lavatory. The colonel tutted and marched into the bar.

'What's up wi' Daviot?' Hamish asked. 'Long car journey?'

'It wasn't any longer than usual, really,' Jimmy said, 'but the snow's fair piling up. The ploughs and gritters are struggling to cope down near Strathbane, let alone up on the high road coming here.'

'Aye, and there's no sign o' it stopping any time soon,' Hamish said. 'Come ben and I'll show you where the body is.'

Jimmy briefly studied the murder scene from the doorway of the breakfast room before sending in the forensic pathologist and a team clad in white overalls from head to foot, who began photographing, scanning and taking samples in the room. Hamish showed Jimmy to the small lounge near the hotel entrance. He had commandeered it as an on-site incident room. In the middle of the room was a table with four chairs and on the table lay the murder weapon, the sword and its scabbard sealed in separate clear-plastic evidence bags. Jimmy carefully picked up the bloodstained sword.

'It's a vicious blade, is it no'?' he said, his hands bouncing gently up and down as he gauged its weight. 'Maybe no' quite as heavy as it looks.'

He replaced the sword on the table and took a seat, asking Hamish to bring him up to date.

'Obviously we secured the murder scene as quick as we could,' Hamish explained, 'but, truth be told, the whole hotel's a crime scene. I've locked it down so that nobody can leave. A few o' the local staff went home as soon as they heard what was going on, but we ken where they bide in the village, so we can talk to them any time.'

'And what about the girl?' Jimmy asked. 'What's happening wi' her?'

'Dr Brodie says she's in shock and needs to rest,' Hamish said. 'Her stepmother and one o' her bridesmaids took her up to her bed, got her undressed and cleaned her up. I've got all her clothes in evidence bags. Her father and her stepmother are sitting by her bed.'

'Good. Put a guard on her door. She was the one who found the body and she was, quite literally, caught red handed. Right from the off we have to consider her our prime suspect.'

'Jimmy, I don't think she's ...' Hamish's objection tailed off when he saw the stern look in the older man's narrow, foxy features. 'Aye, okay. I can ask Silas to guard her door. We need all the serving officers taking statements. We've got a mountain o' interviews to get going on here.'

'Listen, Hamish, I'll be honest wi' you. This couldn't have come at a worse time for me,' Jimmy said in a hushed voice, leaning closer to Hamish even though they were the only two in the room.

'I don't think it came at a particularly good time for anyone here, either,' Hamish pointed out. 'Especially Darius Palmerston.'

'Don't be a smart arse, laddie,' Jimmy said. 'We've a major operation going down afore dawn the morn in Strathbane – three raids that all have to happen at exactly the same time. This is organised crime – extortion, drugs, prostitution, even murder. We've been working on this for months.'

'Is it Gabriel Macgregor's lot again? Is she still pulling strings from behind bars?'

Hamish had had previous run-ins with Glasgow's criminal underworld, one of which had resulted in the head of a major gang being given a lengthy prison sentence.

'Aye, they're involved, but keep all this under your hat. One leak that tips them off and we'll have spent a fortune in resources and manpower for nothing. Everything's in place and it has to happen now.'

'You can rely on me, Jimmy – you ken you can,' Hamish

said with a heavy sigh. 'So this means you're heading back? Well, I can handle everything here, but—'

'It's no' as simple as that,' Jimmy said. 'The forensics team will be pulling out wi' us. We've a van to transport the body as well, but you'll have to seal yon breakfast room. Nobody's to go in there. We'll no' make it back up here until at least Monday morning, and maybe no' even then if the snow keeps up. I can leave you a few o' our uniform lads to help out, but you'll no' be in charge all on your own.'

'So who will be in charge?' Hamish asked, just as Superintendent Daviot walked into the room with what Hamish thought was a peculiarly tentative gait.

'I assume DCI Anderson has been appraising you of the situation in Strathbane,' Daviot said. 'As we can't leave a uniformed sergeant in charge of a murder investigation and we have no senior detectives available, I will be remaining here as the senior investigating officer.'

'Really? You're kidding me!' Hamish's eyebrows shot up towards his hairline. 'How long is it since you've actually handled any kind o' case like this?'

'First of all, *Sergeant* Macbeth,' Daviot said through clenched teeth, 'as a superintendent, I sit three ranks above you and, out of respect for my rank, you *will* call me "sir". There are some important people here and we can't afford to have you making us look like an undisciplined rabble. Is that clear?'

'Aye, I suppose so,' Hamish said reluctantly, quickly adding, '*sir*.'

'That's better,' Daviot said with a curt nod. 'We shall discuss how best to proceed once DCI Anderson and his team have gone. Right now, I have another pressing matter that needs my attention.'

The superintendent left the door ajar, making his way off along the corridor again with the straight-legged, short-striding, buttock-clenched strut of a man who has an urgent appointment with the porcelain.

'Really, Jimmy – what the hell is up wi' him?' Hamish asked.

'How should I ken?' Jimmy replied. 'Curry last night, probably. Touch o' the Delhi belly. You just keep him right, let him take the lead and pick up the phone to me if there's anything I need to know. I'll be back up here wi' murder squad detectives as soon as I can pull them off tomorrow's operation.'

'Aye, right you are, Jimmy,' Hamish said, wearily. 'I'll keep everything running smoothly until then.'

'Time to get moving,' Jimmy said, getting to his feet. 'It's starting to get dark and I want to be back afore yon snow causes us any problems.'

'Well, if you get stuck, give me a call,' Hamish said, grinning, 'and I'll send out my cousin, Callum.'

'Callum . . . ?' Jimmy pondered. 'Aye, I mind o' him all right. Why send him?'

'He's a farmer, Jimmy. He has a great muckle tractor near as big as a house and he bolts the biggest snow plough you've ever seen to the front so that the council will pay him to stand by to help clear the roads.'

'Let's hope it doesn't come to that,' Jimmy said, then pointed to the sword. 'We'll take that thing wi' us.'

Jimmy rounded up his team, all bar four constables he left with Hamish, and the police convoy set off into the gathering gloom, the heavy snow clouds promising an earlier nightfall than Lochdubh had seen of late. Hamish was standing in the hotel entrance, watching them leave, when he heard the heels of the colonel's brogues clicking on the reception area floor and an outraged howl from the hotel owner.

'What the devil's going on?' he demanded. 'Why is the police detail pulling out?'

'Och, you see, Colonel, it's like this,' Hamish said, wondering what on earth he *could* tell the colonel it was like.

'The investigation team has concluded its initial appraisal of the crime scene,' Daviot said, standing by the incident room door. 'They will be back to undertake a more detailed examination once we have the results of various forensic tests.'

It was such a smooth lie that Hamish almost believed it himself, mentally congratulating Daviot on the inventive quality of his blethers.

'Then I have something I simply must discuss with you, Peter,' said the colonel.

'Very well, George,' said Daviot, 'let's take a seat in the incident room. I'd like Sergeant Macbeth to join us.'

'If he must,' tutted the colonel, casting a disparaging glance at Hamish.

'What's so urgent, Colonel?' Hamish asked once they were all seated at the table.

'Well, I hate to speak ill of the dead,' the colonel began, 'but in my mind Darius Palmerston was a complete charlatan!'

'What makes you say that, George?' asked Daviot.

'If he was a British Army cavalry officer, then I'm a son of a haggis!' the colonel exclaimed. Hamish snorted. The colonel glowered at him and carried on. 'He claimed he'd participated in "Trooping of the Colour". That's a hugely important ceremonial occasion to mark the sovereign's birthday. There are almost two thousand on parade and none of them would call it "Trooping *of* the Colour". Everyone in the service calls it "Trooping *the* Colour".'

'That's just a tiny wee slip there, Colonel,' Hamish pointed out.

'No, it isn't, Sergeant – not for an officer in the Household Cavalry,' the colonel maintained, 'but there's more. He claimed he'd spent time training on Salisbury Plain in a Chieftain tank. Complete poppycock! The last of the Chieftains were retired from the British Army in 1996! Palmerston must be around twenty years too young ever to have been anywhere near a Chieftain!'

'Palmerston would have been but a bairn in 1996,' Hamish mused, 'if he was even born at all. I'll check his age.'

'Yes, you do that, Sergeant,' Daviot agreed, looking flustered, beads of sweat breaking on his brow. 'Now you must excuse me. There's something I need to attend to.'

'Wait, Peter – that's not all!' called the colonel, but Daviot had left the room in a hurry. The colonel tutted again and rounded on Hamish. 'Did you take a good look at that sword of his?'

'Aye it looked like a fine piece of craftsmanship,' Hamish said.

'Did you see what was on the hilt?'

'No' really,' Hamish said. 'It was the blade that did the damage, after all. I've some photos o' it here, though.' He reached into a bag under the table and produced his iPad, quickly calling up pictures of the sword.

'Excellent,' said the colonel. 'Now, what can you see on the pommel?'

Hamish looked at the colonel, raised his eyebrows and shrugged, mystified.

'The pommel's the bit at the end of the handle!' the colonel snapped, unable to contain his frustration. 'Look at it – it's a lion's head!'

'Aye, I can see that,' Hamish agreed. 'It's a canny piece o' work right enough.'

'A lion's head pommel identifies this as a Royal Navy officer's sword,' the colonel advised. 'Now look at the engraving on the hand guard. You can see a crown and an anchor motif. That confirms it – this is a naval sword. No cavalry officer would be seen dead on any parade ground with one of those, let alone Trooping the Colour! He'd have been a laughing stock!'

'It seemed to me that his fieldcraft knowledge might have been a bit suspect, too,' Hamish said, recounting for the colonel his discussion with Palmerston about wearing jeans on a snowy hill walk.

'You see!' The colonel clapped his hands in triumph. 'He was an imposter!'

'He was an odd character, no doubt,' agreed Hamish, 'and Elspeth said she was struggling to find service records for him when she was researching him. Leave this wi' me – and let's keep it to ourselves for the time being.'

'Jolly good,' the colonel said, happy that he had at last been taken seriously. 'Mum's the word. We'll keep it strictly hush-hush.'

'Thank you, Colonel,' Hamish said, reaching out to shake the older man's hand. 'Your information might turn out to be very important indeed.'

Hamish crossed the reception area and walked into the bar to see one of Jimmy's young constables finishing taking a statement.

'What's your name, son?' he asked.

'Rory, Sarge,' answered the young man.

'You've still got a car here, have you no', Rory?' Hamish asked.

'Aye, Sarge, I've the keys in my pocket.'

'Good. Take it down to the bridge and send Davey back wi' my Land Rover. He's been out there in the cold long enough. You take ower the roadblock and I'll have someone relieve you in a couple o' hours.'

The young PC grabbed his high-vis waterproof jacket from the seat beside him and left the bar. Hamish surveyed the room. Two of Jimmy's other constables were taking statements at separate tables and he could see through to the dining room where the final Strathbane officer was doing the same. Near the bar sat Richard Wade and Simon Derringer, the two much depleted bottles of Glenfiddich on the table in front of them. Sebastian Chalmers sat with them, his elbows on the table and his head in his hands. Derringer rested a hand on Sebastian's shoulder and Hamish could see, if not hear, that he was offering words of quiet condolence. That much he would have expected to see, but there was something wrong with the melancholy scene. The viscount and Derringer, not having been part of the wedding party, were dressed in the suits they had been wearing all day. Sebastian, on the other hand, had changed out of his Highland regalia. Rather than a Hamilton kilt, he was now wearing jeans and a polo shirt.

'Mr Chalmers,' he said, approaching the group. 'I see you've changed out o' your kilt.'

'Yes,' Sebastian said, looking up. His eyes were red and he'd clearly been crying. 'I couldn't wait to get out of the thing.'

'Why would that be?' Hamish asked.

'I couldn't stand it,' Sebastian said quietly, shaking his

head. 'I never wanted to wear it. I've no right to wear a kilt. I'm not even remotely Scottish.'

'Actually, Chalmers is a grand auld Scots name,' Hamish said. 'Connected wi' royalty, if I mind right. In any case, there are so many thousands o' tartans these days, just about anyone can find some sort o' connection that entitles them to wear a kilt. Many don't bother even trying to find a link and wear one anyway. After all, the kilt's a braw thing to wear for an occasion like today's wedding.'

'Sergeant, I really couldn't give a toss,' Sebastian said, a note of anger in his voice. 'My best friend was just murdered wearing one of those stupid costumes and I couldn't bear to wear it myself a second longer!'

'So where is your wedding outfit now, Mr Chalmers?' Hamish asked.

'It's in my room, of course,' Sebastian replied, then sighed. 'The room I was sharing with Darius.'

'I'll be needing to take a wee look at it,' Hamish said.

'Why the hell do you want to see my clothes?' Sebastian demanded.

'Let's just say you'd be helping me with my enquiries,' Hamish said.

'Have a heart, Sergeant,' Derringer said, patting his friend on the back. 'Poor Seb's had the worst shock of his life. His best friend has just been murdered.'

Sebastian put his face in his hands again and appeared to sob.

'Nevertheless,' Hamish insisted, 'I need you to come wi' me, Mr Chalmers, and show me exactly where you left the clothes you were wearing earlier today.'

'Just do it, Seb,' the viscount said, gently. 'The sergeant's only doing his job and anything that helps him catch whoever did that to Darius is worth it.'

'If you say so.' Sebastian got to his feet, dragged the back of his right hand across his eyes and fished his room key out of his pocket. He led Hamish through the reception area and up the main staircase to the second floor. They were halfway along the corridor when he stopped and pointed to one of the room doors a few feet ahead of them. The door stood slightly open – not fully ajar, merely slightly open in the way that someone in a hurry pulling it shut behind them might not notice it wasn't properly closed.

'That's my room,' Sebastian said, pointing, 'but I didn't leave it like that.'

'Is that right?' Hamish said, swiftly walking past Chalmers and shoving the door open with his elbow. He scanned the room, then waved Chalmers forward. 'There's nobody here. Are you sure you shut the door?'

'Of course I did!' Sebastian snapped, hurrying past Hamish. 'I left my wallet in here ... and my laptop ... and my passport!'

Sebastian checked in a bedside cabinet, and hauled a bag out of a wardrobe, pulling a laptop out before slowly replacing it.

'Everything's here,' he said. 'Nothing's been taken.'

'What about Mr Palmerston's stuff?' Hamish asked.

Sebastian checked the other side of the wardrobe, rifled through a bag and yanked open a drawer in the bedside table.

'I can't be one hundred per cent sure,' Sebastian said, 'but I don't think any of Darius's things are missing.'

'Seems awfy strange that someone would take the risk o' sneaking in here and then no' steal anything,' Hamish said. 'Well, maybe you just didn't shut the door properly after all. Now, can you show me your kilt outfit, please?'

Sebastian looked at his bed then looked at Hamish, shaking his head.

'It was there,' he said. 'I dumped it all right there on the bed – jacket, shirt, waistcoat, kilt, everything! Now it's all gone!'

He skirted the foot of the bed and knelt down to look underneath.

'They've even taken the socks and those bloody silly black brogues that lace halfway up your legs! Somebody's been in here and swiped the lot!'

'Now who would want to be doing that?' Hamish pondered.

'I don't know – you're the policeman, you figure it out!' Sebastian wailed. 'That whole outfit cost over a grand. Maybe one of the locals working at the hotel took it.'

'Aye, maybe . . .' Hamish said, sensing a rising panic in Sebastian's voice.

'I'll tell you something else,' Sebastian said, standing up but still staring at the floor. 'There was a rug right here – a horrible, patterned thing. It's gone, too!'

Hamish looked down at the plain burgundy carpet and could clearly see the outline in the pile confirming the fact that a rug had recently been there. At that moment, his phone rang. It was Davey.

'Hamish, you'd best get down here straight away!' Davey said. There was no mistaking the urgency in his tone.

'Aye, okay, Davey,' Hamish said, heading out into the corridor. 'Where exactly are you?'

'In the gents on the ground floor behind reception,' Davey said. 'I found Daviot in here. He's in a really bad way!'

Hamish dashed down the stairs and along the corridor to find Mr Johnson and Priscilla hovering outside the lavatory door.

'What's happened?' he asked.

'Looks like he collapsed,' Mr Johnson said as Hamish brushed past them.

'Get Dr Brodie back here,' Hamish said.

'Davey's already phoned him,' Priscilla said, by now talking to Hamish's back. 'He's on his way.'

Daviot lay on the lavatory floor, fully dressed in his black uniform tunic, immaculately pressed trousers and polished black shoes. His collar and tie had been loosened and there was a trickle of blood on his cheek from a wound on his temple. His eyes were closed and his skin was so pale that it had a disturbingly green tinge. Davey was kneeling beside him with a first aid kit, holding a sterile pad against the wound.

'He must have hit his head on the urinal when he went down,' Davey said. Daviot groaned and his eyelids flickered but failed to open. Dr Brodie then appeared, stripping off a snow-flecked parka to take over from Davey, who stepped back to the door with Hamish.

'I'd just come in from the bridge,' Davey explained, shifting slightly from foot to foot. 'I needed to pee, so I came in here and there he was. Actually, I still need a . . .'

'Use the ladies, Davey,' Priscilla said, pointing to the door across the corridor. 'There's no one in there.'

Hamish posted Mr Johnson at the end of the corridor to keep any curious guests at bay, then turned when he heard Dr Brodie calling him.

'The bump on his head doesn't look too bad,' the doctor said, 'and he doesn't have any other injuries, but he's obviously very ill.'

'He's had a bad stomach ever since he got here,' Hamish said. 'It was making him look right peely-wally.'

'I want to get him out of here so I can examine him properly,' said Dr Brodie.

As soon as Davey returned, he and Hamish carried Daviot through to the incident room where they laid him on a large sofa. While the doctor unfastened Daviot's tunic to examine him more thoroughly, Davey drew Hamish aside.

'Hamish, I need to talk to you about Alannah Hamilton,' he said quietly. 'I get the feeling this whole wedding might have been a sham.'

'I'm sure you're right,' Hamish said, nodding. 'We'll have a sit-down once we ken what's happening wi' Daviot. In the meantime, take Freddy and do a quick search o' the bins and any other hidey-holes outside the hotel. Sebastian Chalmers's entire wedding outfit has gone missing. I think it might have been dumped, and we need to find it.'

They watched the doctor kneeling by the sofa, examining Daviot, whose head was now neatly bandaged, until he finally dropped his stethoscope into his open medical bag and got to his feet.

'Hamish,' he said, 'I think it's appendicitis. We need to get him to the hospital in Braikie as quick as we can. There's no time to lose.'

'An ambulance will struggle in the snow,' Hamish said, thinking fast, 'and would have to come all the way from Braikie to pick him up. The quickest thing is for me to take him.'

'That's a tricky drive,' Davey said. 'The snow's getting heavier.'

'I ken that road better than anyone,' Hamish said. 'The

Land Rover's got snow tyres and four-wheel drive. I can get him to the hospital faster than anyone else.'

'Right,' said the doctor. 'I'm coming with you.'

'Davey, phone Jimmy,' Hamish said. 'Let him know what's happening. I'll talk to him myself when I get back.'

Minutes later, with Daviot swaddled in blankets and strapped into the rear seat, Dr Brodie at his side, Hamish set off through the falling snow that had now covered the gravel outside the hotel. Davey watched from the hotel entrance, flanked by Mr Johnson and Priscilla.

'In all my years in the hotel business,' said Mr Johnson, 'I've never known a day such as this.'

'I just want all of this to be over,' Priscilla said, then looked to her left, frowning at an empty vase. 'Hey . . . what happened to the roses that were in there?'

Mr Johnson glanced at the vase, rolled his eyes as if he'd been crushed by a final straw and took himself off to the sanctuary of his office.

Chapter Five

The insincerity of man – all men are liars, partial or hiders of facts, half tellers of truths, shirks, moral sneaks. When a merely honest man appears he is a comet . . .

Mark Twain, *Mark Twain's Notebooks*
(published 2015)

Snow was floating lazily down through his headlight beams in big, fluffy flakes, turning the tarmac of Lochdubh's main road white. The road ran along the shore of the loch, protected from the water by the seawall, but with the tang of sea salt hanging almost constantly in the air and forming an invisible coating on the road, it was rare to see any significant accumulation of snow. Over the past week or so, however, Lochdubh had seen its heaviest snow in years and neither the salt nor the grit scattered by the snow ploughs had been enough to fend it off.

'If it's like this down here,' the doctor said, peering out through the windscreen from the back seat, 'it's going to be hell up on the high road.'

'No worries, doctor,' Hamish said, calmly. 'We'll cope.'

At the bridge, the young police officer stood guard, stomping his feet and flapping his arms across his body to keep himself warm. Snow was piling up on his cap. Hamish lowered the window.

'That's it, Rory,' he called as they passed by. 'Good lad! Stay warm and someone will be down to take your place afore you know it!'

Hamish made steady progress climbing out of Lochdubh and, although the snow was deeper when they skirted the moors on the Braikie road, he maintained a respectable speed. The Land Rover's lights easily picked out the snow poles marking the edge of the road. Hamish had lost count of the number of times he'd explained to summer tourists that the tall poles, with red reflectors on one side of the road and white on the other, were there as a guide for drivers on snowy nights such as this.

Although there had been little but a breeze down in Lochdubh, higher up a stiff wind was blowing, sending drifting snow across the road. Hamish pushed on through the smaller drifts and skirted carefully round the deeper ones, all the time checking in his rear-view mirror on the condition of his superintendent, even though the doctor was also keeping a watchful eye on him.

They saw no other traffic until they reached the outskirts of Braikie, no one but those with an urgent need attempting any sort of journey in such heavy snow. On arrival at the hospital, they were met by a doctor and two nurses who transferred Daviot onto a trolley with admirable ease and whisked him through the emergency department, Dr Brodie trotting along behind them.

'Mind and wait for me, Hamish!' he called over his shoulder. 'I'm not staying here tonight!'

Hamish kicked the snow off his boots at the entrance

and walked into the hospital where the nurse behind the reception desk gave him a big smile. Hamish was carrying a large holdall and set it down on the floor.

'You're in luck, Hamish!' said the nurse. 'Claire's handing over a patient in cubicle six – that's the one wi' her paramedic bag outside the curtain. She'll be off shift once she's finished there.'

'Aye, but I've to get back to Lochdubh as soon as I can,' Hamish said. 'Glad she's here, though. I didn't think I'd get to see her tonight.'

They chatted for a few minutes, then the nurse was called away momentarily and seconds later Claire, in her green paramedic overalls, stepped out from behind the cubicle six curtain.

'I knew I could hear your voice!' she said, skipping over and throwing her arms around him. He returned her hug and they kissed, bringing a 'Whoop!' from the nurse who had just returned to reception.

'Och, you're just jealous, Laura!' Claire said, laughing.

'That I am,' Laura admitted. 'A kiss on Valentine's Day. I'll be lucky if I get one o' those!'

'Do you really have to go back?' Claire asked Hamish.

'Aye, lass, I'm afraid I do. I can't very well leave Davey to manage without me.'

'It's such a horrible thing to have happened,' Claire said, shaking her head. 'I can scarcely believe it. The poor girl hadn't been married more than a couple o' hours and she finds her husband . . . like that.'

'It's an awfy mess, right enough. We've a lot o' work to do afore we get to the bottom o' it.'

'You'll sort it out, Hamish. You're Scotland's top cop!'

'Top cop?' he laughed. 'I've no' quite got the salary o' the chief constable, but I'd no' want the job anyway.'

'Well, you're my top cop!' Claire said, and kissed him again.

'Hamish!' Dr Brodie called, appearing through the swing doors leading into the main hospital. 'I'm ready to leave. Don't worry about your boss, he's in good hands here. They'll look after him.'

'Time to go,' Hamish said to Claire and kissed her on the forehead. 'I'll call you when we get back to Lochdubh.'

She stood at the hospital entrance to wave him off, then turned to retrieve her paramedic emergency bag.

'Well, would you look at that!' she said, her face full of delight. Sitting on top of her bag was a pink envelope and a large bunch of red-and-white roses tied with a tartan ribbon.

'You're a lucky girl, Claire,' said Laura. 'Yon Hamish Macbeth's a keeper for sure!'

Hamish was sorry to leave behind the comforting streetlights of Braikie. On the hill road, the darkness made the Land Rover's powerful lights wearingly dazzling when they reflected off the falling snow. When the wind agitated the flakes into a flurry streaming sideways in front them, it all became maddeningly disorientating and he had to slow the car to crawling pace. The visibility became so bad that at no point was he ever able to make anything like normal speed, but the car trundled steadily onwards towards home.

Rounding a bend where he knew there was a rocky outcrop to his left but could barely see it, they hit a short straight stretch of road where the wind was gusting wildly. Having already been reduced to a crawl, he came to a complete halt when he felt the front of the car begin to grind into the snow on the road and then poke its nose into a deeper patch. He and Dr Brodie strained to see through the windscreen, snow settling on the glass as fast as the wiper blades could clear it.

'There's something bad in front of us, Hamish,' the doctor said.

'Aye, that's a high drift,' Hamish replied. He began to lower his window to take a look, but the wind drove a blizzard of snow into the car. On the other side, sheltered from the wind, Dr Brodie was able to open his window and look out.

'It's a huge drift,' he reported, raising his window again, 'almost as high as the car. I can't see how we'll get past that, Hamish. It's right across the road.'

'We have to get past it,' Hamish said, 'or we'll be stuck out here all night!'

'Aye, the way things are going it would take us hours to get back to Braikie, and even then, well . . .'

'Exactly! Even if we could make it back, we'd be in Braikie, which is no' where we need to be! We might no' even get to Braikie if we turn around and come across another drift like this. I'll reverse to the bend,' Hamish decided. 'Maybe we can take a wee run at it and—' His phone began to ring and he pressed a button on the steering wheel to answer it hands free.

'Hamish, where are you?' came a familiar voice.

'Callum!' Hamish said, surprised to get a call from his cousin. 'We're on the Braikie road on our way back to Lochdubh.'

'Are you now?' said Callum. 'On nights like this there's ay a huge drift builds up near the gate to auld Macpherson's top field. Are you anywhere near there?'

'Aye, we drove right into it,' Hamish explained. 'I've just backed up all the way to the bend and—'

'Bide right where you are!' Callum warned. 'Stay well back from yon drift!'

'Callum, what are you talking about?' Hamish asked but there was no reply.

An instant later, Hamish and the doctor were astounded to see the giant snowdrift erupt in a blaze of light, snow scattering in all directions, some clumps even flying far enough to thump into the bonnet of their car. The light then continued towards them before it stopped and the figure of a large man, silhouetted against the brightness, approached the Land Rover.

'Callum!' Hamish yelled, jumping out of the car. 'Man, am I glad to see you!'

The two men embraced and Dr Brodie trudged through the snow to where they were standing, floodlit by the massive lights on the roof of Callum's enormous tractor.

'Jimmy called me,' Callum said. 'He said you were out here and told me to get you back to Lochdubh. Yon drift's ay a monster, but this thing is unstoppable.' He patted the huge snow-clearing blade on the front of the machine.

'I never realised you were friends wi' Jimmy,' Hamish said.

'He arrested me a couple o' times for being drunk and disorderly back in the day,' Callum said, laughing. 'He ay let me off wi' a warning.'

'We'd have been in a right pickle without you,' said the doctor.

'Let's get going then,' Callum said, 'afore we freeze our nuts off! I can turn this beast around just back there, then you can follow me all the way into Lochdubh.'

*

When they arrived back at the Anstey bridge, Hamish was pleased to see a different constable get out of his car to check on them. Clearly, Rory and his pals were taking it in turns. He lowered his window to talk to the officer and was glad that, with almost no wind down by the loch, the snow stayed on the outside.

'Anything happening here?' he asked the constable.

'Not a thing, Sarge,' the young man replied. 'Nothing's come and gone since I've been here and it's been the same for the others.'

'Good,' Hamish said, smiling. 'It's a cold and lonely job, laddie, but someone's got to do it! I'll get someone to bring you down a flask o' tea.'

Hamish dropped Dr Brodie off, then drove up to Tommel Castle. Never had he been so relieved to dismount from the Land Rover. Davey met him at the hotel entrance and they walked through to the dining room together, Hamish letting Davey know all that had happened. He stopped talking abruptly when they entered the dining room.

'What's going on here?' Hamish asked, surprised to see the hotel guests queueing at a long table, Priscilla, Mr Johnson and Freddy serving them supper from an array of stainless-steel catering trays.

'Our guests have to eat, Hamish,' Priscilla said.

'We're keeping everyone well clear of the breakfast room,' Davey pointed out.

'You need to eat, too, Hamish,' Freddy said, grinning. 'I've got some marmalade-glazed gammon here. Grab a plate – you'll love it!'

Hamish and Davey carried their food through to the incident room where they could talk privately.

'Any luck wi' yon missing kilt?' Hamish asked.

'Not yet,' Davey said. 'We checked most of the obvious places but in the dark and with the snow coming down, it seemed sensible to wait until daylight.'

'Aye, you're right,' Hamish said. 'If it's hidden somewhere, it can stay hidden until the morn.'

'I need to talk to you about what I heard yesterday morning outside the stables,' Davey said. 'You know, when Priscilla came to see us in the kitchen . . .'

Davey proceeded to tell Hamish how he had overheard Alannah and Paul talking outside the stables.

'They both sounded really emotional,' Davey explained. 'He said he couldn't believe she was going through with it and "You know what he's like." She said they had to "stick to the plan" and it was "only for one day".'

'They could have been talking about one o' the horses,' Hamish suggested.

'Aye, that's what I thought at the time, but both horses are fit and healthy and they did their jobs faultlessly today. They weren't discussing the horses. By the *tone* of the conversation, I now think they were talking about the wedding and Darius. She said her father would "take care of him".'

'So you say, but he'd surely no' do that on his daughter's wedding day,' Hamish said, frowning and shaking his head. 'According to Elspeth, he's a man who'd do anything to avoid a scandal, and carving up his new son-in-law at the reception when the signatures are barely dry in the church register is something that's going to hit the headlines in all the scuzzy papers.'

'At least we're spared having to deal with the press,' Davey said. 'There's no way any reporters can reach us in this storm. The roads are blocked and I heard Robert

Jensen say that the wind's too strong and visibility's too bad for their helicopter to get here, so we'll have no press flying in either.'

'Aye, we've that to be thankful for. Write down everything you heard Alannah and Paul say, word for word, as soon as you've finished eating,' Hamish said. 'Where's Paul Hunter now?'

'He's got a cosy wee self-contained bedsit arrangement attached to the stables,' Davey said. 'He's out there.'

'Mind if I join you?' Silas said, sticking his head round the door. 'I'd like to have a word wi' the both of you.'

'Aye, come on in, Silas,' Hamish said. 'You might no' be in the police any more, but you did a braw job taking charge o' things in the dining room this afternoon.'

'I surprised myself,' Silas said, chuckling. 'Funny how things you've been trained to do come back to you when you need them.'

Having also brought a plate of food with him, Silas sat at the table and took a mouthful of the gammon.

'Man, that's good,' he said. 'I've no' had a bite to eat since breakfast.'

'What was it you wanted to talk about?' Hamish asked.

'Well, it's just that I don't think the happy couple were actually all that happy together,' Silas said. 'I heard them arguing before the two excursion parties went off yesterday.'

'It's no' unusual for a couple to be a bit tetchy the day afore their wedding,' Hamish pointed out.

'Aye but it felt more serious than that,' Silas went on, 'and then Charles Hamilton seemed to threaten Darius. He told him he had "very little patience with anyone who crosses me". It also seems like Darius wasn't only marrying into the family. He was also to be part of the family business. Sounded like he had a big job that came with this marriage.'

'So the wedding was an even bigger deal for him,' Davey said.

'Aye, you'd think so,' Silas said, 'but at the wedding reception, he came into the bar along wi' Serena Hamilton and I saw him, plain as day, give her arse a squeeze! I thought she would batter him, but she gave him a wee smile! They came through from the dining room. I'd seen them use that route on Thursday as well. They could easily have just come down the backstairs. Actually, I think that's exactly where they *did* come from. I've seen that look on people's faces afore. You do a lot o' people-watching working in a hotel and you get to know the signs. They looked to me like they'd been upstairs for a spot o' hanky-panky.'

'Are you saying he shagged his stepmother-in-law as soon as he got back from his wedding in the church?' Davey said, flabbergasted.

'That's definitely what it looked like to me,' Silas maintained.

'In the name o' the wee man,' Hamish said, setting down his knife and fork and running his hands through his hair. 'Is there anyone in this family who's on the level?'

'Seems not,' Silas said. 'One o' Jimmy's lads is covering for me outside Alannah's room right now but when I was sitting there earlier, I heard whispering from inside. That was weird because Alannah was in there on her own, so I pressed my ear against the door. I couldn't hear what she was saying but I definitely heard her say the name "Paul". I think she was talking on her phone to the lad out in the stables.'

'Did I no' ask Priscilla to collect everybody's phones?' Hamish said.

'Aye, but Alannah would have been in no condition to hand over her phone and passcode,' Davey said, 'and Paul had gone back out to the stables, so she must have forgotten about him.'

'So it would seem,' Hamish said, pausing for a second when he felt his temper warming the back of his neck. He was annoyed that two phones had slipped through the net, especially as Priscilla was normally so efficient in everything she did. On the other hand, she'd just had a dreadful shock and seen the wedding she'd spent so long planning turn into a total disaster. It was hardly surprising that she wasn't on top form. 'Davey, get out to the stables, make sure Paul Hunter is still there and get his phone off him. Silas, you and I can pay Alannah a visit and get hold o' her phone. I'd like to have a wee word wi' her and if she's well enough for sneaky phone calls, then she's well enough to talk to me.'

'Can I have my marmalade gammon first?' Silas asked.

'Aye,' Hamish said, picking up his knife and fork to finish off his own helping. 'This is far too good to let it go to waste.'

Five minutes later, Hamish and Silas were making their way up the main staircase to the first floor.

'Silas, I'm going to need your help to find whoever killed Darius Palmerston,' Hamish said. 'You ken all the folk involved. You have lists o' all the guests and you can get me a list o' everyone who was working here today.'

'Aye, that's easy enough,' Silas said, 'but should you no' just wait until Jimmy and his lads can get back?'

'The trail, as they say, will be cold by then,' Hamish replied. 'We can do some valuable work now to give the murder squad a head start when they get back. The more evidence we can gather, the better. In any case,' he added, sounding resentful, 'this happened on my patch right under my nose. If we can nail the scunner who did this, we can avoid having a load o' cops from down in Strathbane blundering around the village upsetting folk.'

'That's a pretty tall order,' Silas commented. 'Tracking down a murderer so quickly after the crime isn't usually the way things work.'

'No, it's no',' Hamish agreed, 'but we have one big advantage. We don't have to track anyone very far. I've no doubt the murderer is still here in Lochdubh. In fact, I'd bet whoever killed Darius Palmerston is still right here in the hotel.'

As the bride, and given that she would need plenty of space to prepare for her big day, her bridesmaids helping with her hair and making sure her dress was perfect, Alannah had a room to herself on the first floor. Walking along the corridor with Silas, Hamish could see the young PC, Rory, seated outside Alannah's door.

'Is there anyone in there with her, Rory?' Hamish asked.

'Aye, Sarge,' he replied. 'Her bridesmaid Helen Carter is sitting with her.'

'Has anyone else been in to see her?' Hamish asked.

'Only her father and stepmother,' Rory reported. 'Davey said no one else was to be allowed in – just them and the bridesmaids. She's had one other visitor who's been turned away twice . . .' he pulled out his notebook and flipped the pages, '. . . Paul Hunter. He was quite insistent, but I wouldn't let him in.'

'Well done, Rory. Best you bide here, Silas,' Hamish said before tapping gently on the door. He heard a voice telling him to come in and pushed the door open.

The spacious room was lit only with a lamp on a chest of drawers near what Hamish could see was the door to an en suite bathroom. There was a large wardrobe against one wall and a dressing table nestled in a bay window. The curtains were closed. Alannah lay in a double bed that was flanked by two bedside cabinets. She was lying on her back and looked like she might have been asleep, save for the fact that her eyes were open, staring at the ceiling. Her bridesmaid, Helen Carter, still wearing her dark green bridesmaid's dress with a rose corsage on a backing of Hamilton tartan pinned just below her left shoulder, was sitting at her bedside.

'How is she?' Hamish asked softly, almost ashamed to disturb the silence in the room.

'"She" is awake, Sergeant,' Alannah said, turning her head towards him.

'How are you feeling?' he asked.

'How do you think I feel?' she said, her eyes narrowing with rage. 'No, don't even bother to answer that! How could you ever hope to understand how I'm feeling? How could you possibly know?'

'I know because I've seen this many times before,' he said, gently. 'I've seen folk broken wi' grief more times than I care to remember. I've seen violence and death and had to help those left behind get on wi' their lives ... but most o' all, I know because it happened to me. My fiancée was killed on our wedding day and I was the one who found her body. I've never known a feeling like it and I'm feeling it again right now standing here talking to you. I thought the pain would be too much to bear. What should have been the most glorious day o' my life turned into my darkest nightmare. It near drove me mad and it's something I'll never be able to put behind me. That's how I know. I have been where you are now.'

'I'm ... sorry,' she said and reached her hand across the bed towards him. He sat in a chair opposite the bridesmaid and took her hand.

'That's all right, lass,' he said. 'It's an awfy thing to have in common and I'm no' going to bother you wi' it all now. Try to get some rest and maybe we can talk again in the morn. In the meantime, we're working hard to find out who did this. It would help me if you could let me have your phone. I'll no' need it for long but I can't stress how important it might be.'

'But how can my phone help?' she asked.

'It might not,' he told her, 'but I won't know that till I take a look. You can be sure that everything on it that's personal or private will remain just that.'

'Give him it,' Alannah said with a resigned sigh, looking towards the phone on her bedside cabinet. Helen handed Hamish the phone and Alannah recited her passcode, which he wrote on a slip of paper, dropping both into an evidence bag.

'They won't let me see Paul,' Alannah said, a tear forming in the corner of her eye. 'I need to see Paul.'

'I'll talk to your father about that,' he said, patting her hand. 'Everyone will have told you to try to rest and they're no' wrong. Rest. You need to get your strength back.' He was leaving the room when he heard Helen behind him.

'Sergeant, can I speak with you, please?' the young woman said, following him out into the corridor and closing the door behind them. She then hesitated, glancing at Silas and Rory.

'Give us a minute, would you, lads?' Hamish asked, and the two men strolled off towards the staircase. He looked down at the young woman, although she stood tall enough to gaze back at him with barely a tilt of her head. She was pretty, with long waves of black hair, fair skin and deep blue eyes.

'You're still wearing your wedding outfit,' he noted.

'Yes. I wanted to get changed,' she said, 'but Alannah said no. She said I looked beautiful and that this was the dress I was meant to be wearing all day today. She wanted me to wear it. I don't think she was thinking straight at the time but, well, I didn't want her getting any more upset.'

'Quite right,' Hamish said. 'Now what was it you wanted to tell me?'

'I'm worried about Sloane, the other bridesmaid,' Helen said. 'She hasn't been to see Alannah and I don't know where she is.'

'She must be as distressed as everyone else,' Hamish said. 'Maybe she just wants to be alone. She's probably in her room.'

'Sloane never wants to be alone. She's one of those people who always likes to have friends around her. She always has to be with someone,' Helen said. 'And we share a room. Last time I checked she wasn't there.'

'She must still be in the hotel. Who might she be with?'

'I'm not sure. She can be a bit of a flirt and she was out to get a man this weekend. She even took a shine to Seb. If she was with someone, though ... you know, for a bit of comfort, a shoulder to cry on ... even then, she would still have come to check on Alannah before now. The three of us are best friends. She would want to be with Alannah and me right now.'

'When was the last time you saw her?' Hamish asked.

'She was at the top table during the wedding meal,'

Helen said, 'but then, with everything that happened, it all gets a bit confusing.'

'Don't worry, miss,' Hamish said. 'We'll have a look for her. When we find her, I'll let you know. You bide wi' Alannah in the meantime.'

Hamish strode along the corridor towards Silas and Rory.

'Rory, park your arse back on yon chair,' he said. 'If Sloane Beaumont shows up looking to see Alannah, you contact me immediately. Clear?'

'Aye, Sarge,' Rory said, trotting back to his post.

'Silas, come wi' me.'

Hamish then thumbed the radio dangling from the shoulder of his Police Scotland sweater.

'Davey, where are you now?'

'Incident room,' came Davey's reply.

'Bide there. We're on our way.'

In the incident room, Davey was sitting at the table piled with mobile phones in plastic bags. He pointed to a grey metal cabinet against the wall.

'Mr Johnson had that in his office,' Davey explained. 'We brought it through here because I thought we could use it to lock away all these until we start looking at them.'

'That's grand,' Hamish said, nodding. 'Lock them all away for now. Where are Jimmy's other men?'

'One's down at the bridge and the other two are having a kip,' Silas said. 'I let them use my quarters. They've been on duty since six this morning.'

'Fine,' Hamish said, sitting at the table. 'Let them rest. We'll need them to take turns mounting guard through the night. Right now we have another problem – Sloane Beaumont has gone missing.'

'You mean she's run off?' Davey asked, stacking phones in the cabinet. 'In this weather?'

'Aye,' Hamish agreed, 'you'd need a powerful reason to want to go out on a night like this, would you no'? It's the sort o' thing a murderer on the run might try.'

'You think she killed Palmerston?' Davey said.

'If she did, then she's not left the building,' Silas said. 'I locked all the exit doors and the windows. It's strictly against fire regulations, of course, but the only way out is through the main entrance. Mr Johnson has been letting staff going home leave that way and locking the door behind them.'

'That's right,' Davey confirmed. 'He had to let me out that way and I had to go right round the building to see Paul Hunter.'

'The main entrance and reception area is covered by a security camera,' said Silas, 'and there are others on the outside of the building.'

'They're monitored from Mr Johnson's office, are they no'?' Hamish asked Silas, who nodded. 'We'll get him to go back through the footage to see if she managed to sneak out somehow.'

'Could she really have swung that sword and then stabbed it into Palmerston?' Davey seemed unconvinced. 'Would she have been strong enough?'

'We'll ask her when we find her, Davey,' Hamish replied. 'She's likely still here in the hotel, so we need to mount a search, but I don't want to cause a panic. What are the guests up to right now, Silas?'

'A few are still in the dining room or the bar. Most have already gone up to their rooms. It's getting late now and today's been . . . exhausting.'

'Okay,' Hamish said firmly, having decided what to

do. 'Davey, you check the public areas down here, then go through the security camera footage wi' Mr Johnson. Silas, we'll find Priscilla and go from room to room.'

Priscilla was sitting in Mr Johnson's office, looking grim and clearly having a serious conversation with the hotel manager.

'What's up?' said Hamish as he walked into the room.

'Oh, nothing much,' Priscilla said, looking up at him, wide-eyed, 'apart from the facts that a man was butchered in our breakfast room, my parents are so distraught they won't leave their apartment, the business is probably ruined and we have a murderer somewhere in the building!'

'Aye, well, I hate to add to your list o' worries, but we also have a missing guest – Sloane Beaumont,' Hamish explained. 'I need you to help us search room to room, but we might want some sort o' excuse so as no' to throw everyone into a panic.'

'Right,' Priscilla said, reaching out to grab a passkey from a cupboard. 'Let's get going.'

Almost as if she was pleased to be doing something active and positive, Priscilla suggested they start on the top floor. The first room was unoccupied and she took Silas in with her while Hamish hovered outside in the corridor. There was a young couple in the next room and Priscilla apologised for disturbing them but said they were looking for a leak.

'There's water coming through the ceiling below,' she explained. 'It's the Victorian plumbing, you see. Some of it is in dire need of replacement.'

So it continued – Priscilla checked in bathrooms and Silas crawled on the floor, maintaining he was checking radiators and listening for leaks but actually peering under beds. There was no sign of Sloane. When they reached the first-floor corridor, the first door Priscilla knocked on was one of the larger rooms, almost a suite, occupied by Charles Hamilton and his wife, Serena. She opened the door and, sitting in armchairs by a fireplace, Hamish could see her husband with Robert Jensen, both drinking generous measures of whisky. Priscilla and Silas were invited in to 'check for leaks' and Hamilton stared out at Hamish.

'What are you doing lurking out there, Sergeant?' he called. 'Come in, man, we don't bite!'

'I'm just walking around the hotel wi' Silas and Priscilla,' he said. 'After what happened – the murder – we've no real reason to expect there will be any more unpleasantness, but we're keeping an eye on everything nonetheless.'

'You're patrolling the corridors?' Jensen asked.

'Keeping the guests and the staff safe,' Hamish replied.

'Safe from whom, though, Sergeant?' Hamilton frowned. 'No one has any idea who did that to Darius, do they?'

'We're working on it,' Hamish said. 'We've taken initial statements from just about everyone here today and we'll be following up wi' further enquiries.'

'Surely there were fingerprints on that damned sword?' Jensen asked.

'Aye, plenty o' prints,' Hamish agreed. 'Too many, in fact. It was a dandy thing, yon sword, and it looks like near everyone in the place took a hold of it at some time. They're sorting out the individual prints now and it might then be necessary to fingerprint everyone here who handled it.'

'My daughter needs to be at home where she feels safe.

When will we be able to get out of this bloody place?' Hamilton demanded.

'That remains to be seen,' Hamish said, stepping back out into the corridor as Priscilla and Silas finished their inspection. 'At the moment, we're snowed in, so you're stuck here anyway.'

There was no sign of Sloane in any of the other rooms and they reconvened with Davey and Mr Johnson in the hotel office, meeting Freddy in the corridor outside.

'I've got my last four local kids finishing the cleaning up in the kitchen,' Freddy said. 'Anything I can help you wi' out here?'

Hamish thought for a moment. As a former police officer, Freddy, like Silas, would be a useful asset throughout whatever was to come during the night.

'Aye, Freddy,' he said. 'Davey, let Freddy have the Land Rover keys. Make sure all your folk get home safe, Freddy, then report back here. I've the feeling we're going to need all the help we can get.'

Hamish, Davey, Silas, Mr Johnson and Priscilla all crowded into the small office, standing, sitting on desks or chairs, or leaning against filing cabinets wherever they could fit.

'We've run through all the camera footage,' Davey said. 'We did it on fast forward from the time the wedding party arrived back at the hotel. We didn't see anybody that could be Sloane leaving the building.'

'So she's still here,' Hamish said, 'but because we couldn't find her in any o' the rooms in a normal way, we now have to look again. This time, though, either we're looking for somebody who's determined to hide from us, or—'

'We're looking for a corpse,' Elspeth, standing in the office doorway, finished the sentence for him.

'Do you know something we don't?' Hamish looked at her with raised eyebrows.

'If you mean the gift, then no,' Elspeth told him, 'but I overheard you earlier and if Sloane's disappeared, then those options are obvious. I want to help.'

'Good,' Hamish said. 'Elspeth, get a coat on and get out to the stables and Paul Hunter's wee pad wi' Davey. Make sure she's no' out there. Silas, start looking in any storage spaces or cubby holes on the ground floor and check the kitchens wi' Freddy when he gets back. Mr Johnson, keep an eye on yon TV screens and make sure no one leaves the building. Priscilla, you and I will start at the top o' the house.'

Hamish and Priscilla trotted up the main staircase to the top floor where Hamish looked up at the corridor ceiling.

'How do we get into the attic spaces?' he asked.

'There aren't really any attics,' Priscilla informed him. 'Where we're standing was once part of the attic. The rest was converted into the smaller hotel rooms we checked earlier.'

Hamish pointed to a door that was different from the normal room doors.

'Where does that go?' he asked.

'Out onto the roof,' Priscilla replied, examining a bunch of keys she had brought with her. She selected one and unlocked the door. Hamish opened it to find a short flight of stairs to another door for which Priscilla also provided a key. He turned the lock and pulled it open only to be met by the howl of the wind and clods of built-up snow that tumbled down onto the stairs. He squinted outside, then slammed the door shut again.

'Nobody's been out there,' he said, wiping melting

snow from his face. 'The snow's no' been disturbed. No footprints – nothing.'

They locked the doors and, once back in the corridor, Hamish pointed out another door that was also different from those of the regular rooms.

'It's basically a broom cupboard,' Priscilla explained, unlocking the door and flicking a light switch. 'There's one on each floor. It has room to store a vacuum cleaner and other essentials.'

Hamish took a look inside, nodded, and they proceeded downstairs. It wasn't until they reached the second-floor broom cupboard that Priscilla noticed something strange.

'The door's not locked,' she said, trying the key. She turned the handle, swung the door open and frowned. 'That shouldn't be there.'

Hamish looked into cupboard to see a rolled rug standing on end.

'There was a rug missing from Chalmers's room,' he said, grabbing hold of it. 'Let's take a proper look at it.'

He hauled on the top of the roll but found it far heavier than he expected and stumbled backwards slightly, still grasping the rug's edge. The rug unrolled in the corridor and suddenly there, on the floor in front of them, still wearing her dark green bridesmaid's dress, was the body of Sloane Beaumont.

Chapter Six

The Bustle in a House
The Morning after Death
Is solemnest of industries
Enacted upon Earth
   Emily Dickinson, 'The Bustle in a House' (published 1890)

Hamish crouched to feel for a pulse but could find no signs of life. There were bloodstains on the rug and on a bath towel that had been rolled up with the body. He saw that Sloane's hair was matted with blood and moved her sideways slightly to find a massive wound on the back of her head.

Priscilla slumped against the wall then slid down onto the floor, unable to take her eyes off the body of her friend. She was trembling and tears were rolling down her face.

'Priscilla,' Hamish said calmly, squatting in front of her and taking her hands. 'Listen to me. I ken this is horrible for you, but we can't leave her there. I want to get her out o' the corridor afore anyone else sees her.'

'That's her room,' Priscilla whispered, pointing to one of the doors and holding out her passkey.

Hamish took the key, opened the door and dragged the rug, with the body still lying on it, into the room. He then clicked his radio and spoke quietly.

'Davey, are you finished outside? Aye, well come straight up to the second floor. I need you to make sure no one goes into one o' these rooms.'

He then called Dr Brodie.

'I'm afraid I need you here again, Doctor, quick as you can,' he said. 'It's a fatality but I'm trying to keep a lid on this for the time being. Let me know when you're outside and we'll bring you straight up to where the body is.'

With Davey in the corridor, guarding the room door, Hamish assembled his team in the incident room. Elspeth sat with Priscilla, who was sobbing gently, wiping her eyes and blowing her nose, a box of tissues by her side. Hamish closed the door.

'Once Dr Brodie gets here, he will make the official pronouncement,' Hamish said, and Priscilla wept a little harder. Elspeth put her arm around her. 'We will then wait until the coast's clear and get the body out of the hotel. The doctor has a temporary mortuary at his place. I don't want anyone outside this room knowing that there's been another murder. If folk panic and start trying to get out of here, things could go very badly. I'll have officers patrolling the corridors all night, so once everyone's in their rooms wi' their doors locked, they're all safe.'

There was a knock at the door and Hamish, expecting Dr Brodie, opened it. Helen Carter stood in the corridor.

'Your constable wouldn't let me into my room,' she said. 'He told me to come and see you.'

'Come in, Miss Carter,' he said, closing the door behind her. 'The thing is, there's evidence in your room that we need to preserve, so we can't let you in, but—'

'Priscilla!' Helen said, rushing over to her friend when she saw her crying. 'What's wrong? Why are you . . . ? Oh, no!' She looked at Hamish, her face pale when she realised what was happening. 'It's Sloane, isn't it? You've . . . found her.'

'Aye, lass,' Hamish said. 'You'd best take a seat.'

Hamish explained that he and Priscilla had found Sloane's body, whereupon Helen and Priscilla collapsed into each other's arms. Mr Johnson then appeared with Dr Brodie.

'This is a terrible business, Hamish,' the doctor said.

'It is, Doctor,' Hamish agreed. 'I'll take you up in a second. Silas, is anybody left downstairs?'

'Richard Wade, Simon Derringer and Sebastian Chalmers are the last in the bar,' Silas said. 'The bar staff went home a while ago, so I've been standing in.'

'Once we go upstairs,' said Hamish, 'close the bar. Send Wade and Derringer up to their room. Chalmers is a problem. We need to keep his room out o' bounds – and Miss Carter's room, for that matter.'

'There are no other rooms,' Mr Johnson pointed out. 'They're all allocated.'

'Helen can stay with me in the private apartment,' Priscilla said.

'Good,' Hamish said. 'I want to keep an eye on Chalmers, so he can bed down on the sofa in here. Silas, I want you and Mr Johnson on guard on the ground floor. Freddy, you go up and keep an eye on the top floor. Davey's on the second floor and young Rory's on the first. I'll draw up a rota to include Jimmy's other three constables so we can all get some shuteye, but we'll all have to do our stints on guard duty through the night. We need to keep our wits about us – I don't think I need to remind you that there's a murderer in the hotel.'

'I . . . I need to say goodnight to Richard before he goes upstairs,' Helen announced.

'Lass, I don't know if I can . . .' Hamish began, hesitating when he saw her wiping her eyes and straightening her dress.

'I won't tell him anything,' she said. 'I'll say that Priscilla's exhausted and upset and that I want to sit with her. That's not exactly a lie, really, is it?'

'No, I suppose it's no',' Hamish agreed, wondering why the young woman needed to talk to the viscount at all.

Once all the guests were in their rooms and Dr Brodie had examined the body, Hamish and Davey carried the corpse downstairs in a body bag and out to the Land Rover. Hamish paused for a moment as they passed the incident room. Chalmers had been bumbling drunk when he'd collapsed on the sofa and had gone out like a light. There were no sounds from inside and Hamish had subtly locked the door from the outside to make sure that Chalmers stayed right where he was.

As soon as they got back from the surgery, Hamish sat in the bar with a cup of coffee and phoned Jimmy. He sounded groggy when he answered.

'What's happening?' he asked, yawning loudly. 'I was just trying to get forty winks here afore the whole show kicks off.'

'Jimmy, there's been another murder,' Hamish said, then recoiled from his phone as Jimmy's response turned the air blue with the sort of profanities he hadn't heard since the day he arrested four drunken Glasgow Rangers supporters trying to stage a race along the shore road, two pushing and two crammed inside tractor tyres. Once Jimmy had calmed down, he ran through all that had happened.

'Dr Brodie couldn't give me a very accurate time o' death for Sloane Beaumont, but his best estimate is that it happened roughly around the same time Palmerston was killed. That ties in wi' the last time she was seen by Helen Carter.'

'How are the rest o' the hotel guests taking it?' Jimmy asked.

'None o' them know about Sloane – except for the murderer, of course,' Hamish explained. 'Everybody is now tucked up in their rooms and I've got Chalmers locked in the incident room. I'll be in there wi' him shortly. He's out for the count. His pals Wade and Derringer got him pie-eyed.

'Obviously, he's a suspect, but so is Alannah Hamilton, her father, Paul Hunter and goodness knows who else. I'll know more when I start talking to them in the morn.'

'You be careful how you handle these folk, laddie,' Jimmy warned him. 'Charles Hamilton is a powerful man and his pal Robert Jensen is one o' yon media barons – they could bring a whole world o' trouble down on our heids. Then there's the viscount and . . .'

'Aye, Jimmy, I get it, but we have to be seen to be doing something. Even if you had the men available, we're snowed in and you'll no' be able to get here until the weather breaks. I'll talk to you once your big raids are ower and done wi'.'

Hamish went to the bar to pour himself a coffee refill, then sat at a table and opened his laptop. He needed to know more about Darius and Sebastian. He began by looking for criminal records, making notes and moving on to look for any records of their military service. Having garnered some basic details, he closed his laptop and went to check on Sebastian, who was sound asleep. He locked the incident room door again and made his way upstairs to the second floor, where he met Davey.

'I'm going to take a wee look around the room Palmerston and Chalmers shared,' he said, pulling on a pair of latex gloves. 'Keep your eyes peeled and let me know if you see or hear anything.'

Davey nodded and Hamish let himself into the room. He looked at the carpet where the rug had been. Examining it closely, there were traces of what he was sure was blood and marks where attempts had been made to scrub the carpet. There were also marks on the wardrobe door where it, too, had been wiped clean. He had no doubt that this was the scene of Sloane Beaumont's murder. He found Sebastian's laptop. There could be all manner of things on the slim computer that might point to Sebastian being the killer, but he'd need Sebastian to provide the relevant passcode. He set it down on the chest of drawers and went through the wardrobe and the bedside cabinets, finding nothing that seemed suspicious.

Spotting some torn paper in the waste basket, he fished out a pale yellow envelope and a Valentine's card. He pieced the envelope together on the bed to reveal the letter 'D'. The card, it would appear, had been given to Darius. He took out his phone to photograph the envelope, then worked on the jigsaw of torn fragments that was the card.

The front of the card matched the yellow of its envelope and had a large, red heart shape with the words 'For my Valentine' printed in yellow. He photographed the outside then turned the pieces over to find a handwritten message inside saying 'All my love, S.' On the morning of his wedding, Darius had received a Valentine's card that clearly was not from his bride-to-be. Who might 'S' be? Silas was convinced that Darius was having an affair with Serena. Had she been so indiscreet as to slip a card under his door? On the other hand, Sloane had been murdered in this room. Had Darius been playing her along as well? And why had the card been ripped up?

Dropping the fragments of card and envelope into an evidence bag, he took a last look around. There was nothing that he could see might have been used as the murder weapon. Dr Brodie's only comment was that it must have been something heavy that would have been swung with great force. Nothing in the room really fitted the bill. He looked in the bathroom, noting that, as he'd expected, one of the bath towels was missing. He left the room, locked the door and checked with Davey that his guard duty rota was all set up. Then he went back downstairs to the incident room.

Sebastian was snoring on the sofa. Hamish stared at him for a few moments. Could this man really be a double murderer? Things certainly looked bad for him. The clothes he had been wearing at the wedding had disappeared. Had he disposed of them because they were spattered with Palmerston's blood? Could he really have bludgeoned Sloane, rolled her in the rug and hidden her body in the broom cupboard? The man was, perhaps, an odd character, but was he a callous killer? If he was, what had led him to murder both his best friend and an innocent young woman?

Hamish shook his head, feeling a wave of fatigue sweeping over him. He locked the torn card in the metal cabinet, picked up his laptop and returned to the bar, locking Sebastian in the incident room. The thought of yet more coffee left him cold, so he helped himself to a small measure of Glenmorangie. That, he had no doubt, would help him concentrate on the research he was about to undertake on his computer.

He woke to the sound of Mr Johnson gently shaking his shoulder. The laptop was still open on the table in front of him but had gone into sleep mode, just as he had done.

'Sergeant Macbeth, the guests will start appearing for breakfast in less than an hour,' Mr Johnson said.

'Aye, come on, Hamish,' Davey said, 'Rise and shine! I've just popped back to the station for a shower and a change o' clothes. You should do the same. It's not bad outside. It's getting light and the snow's just stopped.'

'A shower would be a good . . .' Hamish yawned and stretched, then a panicked look crossed his face. 'Wait a minute! The snow's stopped?'

He dashed for the front door, plucking his phone from his pocket.

'Jimmy!' he said when his call was answered. 'The snow's stopped!'

Half an hour later, he was back, showered, refreshed and wearing a clean shirt. The first people he saw when he walked into the hotel were Priscilla and Helen.

'Good morning, ladies,' he said, smiling. Neither of them shared his enthusiasm for the new day. 'Can I have a quick word wi' you both, please?'

They stood together in the bar area where Hamish kept his voice low, even though there was no one else around.

'We need to keep the whole business about Sloane quiet for the time being,' he said.

'We can't hide the fact that she's missing,' Priscilla said. 'Some of the others are bound to wonder where she is.'

'Aye, but if anyone asks, maybe you could say you think she might be in her room, or in wi' Alannah, or getting a breath o' fresh air,' Hamish said. 'It's just for a wee while. I don't want folk panicking and trying to leave the village. There's no safe way to do that right now. By later today, we'll have more police here and we'll be able to manage things better.'

'Are we in danger here, Sergeant?' Helen looked seriously concerned. 'I think that's what everyone really wants to know. People are scared.'

'I don't think anyone need worry too much, miss,' he said, sounding solidly confident. 'The two murders are obviously linked but I doubt there will be another. In the meantime, we'll have officers in the hotel to keep everyone safe, but I will be asking all of the guests to stay in their rooms today except, perhaps, for mealtimes.'

'I'll make sure they all get the message,' Priscilla said. 'I can also make sure we're operating with a skeleton staff. We'll have as few outsiders as possible in the building.'

'Thanks, Priscilla, that would be grand,' Hamish said, and she hurried off to check that breakfast was underway. 'In the meantime, miss,' Hamish said to Helen, 'I ken you must be feeling pretty low right now, but I need to ask you a few questions.'

'What sort of questions?' she asked.

'Well, I'd like to know more about Darius and his life down south. You were friends wi' him.'

'I was friends with Sloane and Alannah. I got to know Priscilla through work and she became part of our group. I would never really have counted Darius as a proper friend. If you want to know more about him, you should ask Priscilla.'

'Why Priscilla?'

'They were close once.'

'Very well,' Hamish said. 'I'll do that, but can I also ask you why you were so keen to say goodnight to Viscount Carsely last night?'

'I . . . I'm sorry, Sergeant,' Helen said, looking at the floor. 'I can't answer any more questions right now. You must excuse me, please.'

With that, she marched off into the reception area and down the corridor, heading for the sanctuary of the ladies' lavatory. Hamish ran a hand through his hair. To him, Helen Carter seemed like a decent, honest young woman. So what was it that she was trying to hide? He shook his head as though some bright nugget of inspiration might break loose, then wandered over to the incident room. Davey and Sebastian were waiting there for him.

'What's going on, Sergeant?' Sebastian demanded. 'Am I under arrest?'

'What makes you think you should be under arrest?' Hamish asked.

'I . . . well . . . of course I don't think I should be,' Chalmers said, frowning, 'but your constable here doesn't seem to want to let me out of his sight. He practically frogmarched me upstairs to the hotel security man's apartment to shower and change. He fetched clothes from my room and now I'm back in here.'

'Your room is quarantined until the investigation team returns later today,' Hamish informed him, staring into Sebastian's bloodshot eyes. 'I'll be wanting to have a wee word wi' you later, once your hangover's worn off, but in the meantime the best thing for you is a good breakfast. Constable Forbes probably needs a bite to eat as well.'

'I do that,' Davey agreed.

'Then you two should get yourselves off to the dining room,' Hamish advised and, just before Davey could follow Sebastian out into reception, he caught his eye. 'Good work, Davey. Keep an eye on him.'

Hamish noticed a clutch of 'Tommel Castle' branded umbrellas propped in a corner of the room, clearly ready as back-ups for the ones kept in the reception area for guests to use. He picked one up and hefted it to test its balance, then held it out like a sword. He was swinging, slashing and stabbing with it when Silas walked in.

'Careful wi' that!' Silas laughed. 'We don't want to have to call Dr Brodie back again!'

'Aye, he's seen enough o' Tommel Castle to last him a lifetime,' Hamish agreed, laying the umbrella down on the metal evidence cabinet. 'Look at this, though, Silas. Let's say yon cabinet is the cake table and the umbrella is Palmerston's sword. Now, you stand here.'

Silas put down the papers he was carrying and allowed Hamish to pose him by the cabinet.

'The thing is, I've been wondering about the way Palmerston's body was lying,' Hamish explained, turning his back on Silas and taking a step forward. 'Now, imagine I'm walking away from you. You take the sword and brandish it up high. I see the movement out o' the corner o' my eye and turn round.'

Hamish turned.

'You then slash at me wi' the sword and get me across the neck.'

Silas swung the umbrella in slow motion until it was touching Hamish's neck.

'The force o' the blow, the shock and the pain send me right to the floor,' Hamish said, lowering his lanky frame onto the carpet. 'Because I was turning, my legs end up crossed, and because I had no time even to raise my arms, they are by my sides wi' no defensive wounds. Then you step forward, stand ower me.'

Silas did as Hamish described, straddling Hamish, who lay on the floor looking up at him.

'The first wound alone would have been fatal,' he said. 'That's where the blood spatter on the table and the cake came from. The murderer would also have been hit wi' that blood. Palmerston would have been in no condition to put up any fight. You then plunge the sword into my chest.'

Silas held the umbrella in both hands, its tip balanced on Hamish's chest.

'It's all happened in only a second,' Hamish said. 'Palmerston would have been taken by surprise and wouldn't even have had time to cry out, so no one in the dining room next door heard a thing above the din o' their own chattering. What do you think?'

'I lifted that sword and it wasn't too heavy,' Silas said. 'Once you had it in the air, slashing down wouldn't be difficult. Stabbing it into someone who was standing would take a bit more strength, but standing here and pushing down with all my weight behind it would be easy. Anyone could do it.'

'That's what I was thinking,' Hamish agreed. 'Palmerston's killer could be anyone – a man or a woman.'

'What on earth are you two up to?' Priscilla said, walking into the room carrying a plate with a stack of well-stuffed bacon rolls.

'A re-enactment,' Silas explained, stepping back and offering Hamish his hand to heave him up off the floor. 'Working out how the deed was done.'

'Really?' Priscilla said with a tortured sigh, as though she'd just discovered two grubby little boys playing some silly game. 'I thought you might need something to eat. Elspeth is bringing some coffee.'

They sat around the table, Hamish, Silas and Elspeth tucking into bacon rolls, Priscilla quietly sipping her coffee.

'Hamish, what I really came to talk to you about was this.' Silas offered Hamish the papers he had brought with him. 'Davey and I went through the initial statements and I've been able to draw up these lists. The first is a list of everyone we know who was in the hotel at the time of Palmerston's murder. The second list is everyone who was with two or more others at that time.'

'That's grand, Silas,' Hamish said, scanning the list. 'Wi' two or more to vouch for them, they're pretty much out o' the running as suspects.'

'The third list is those who had only one other person with them,' Silas explained.

'Charles Hamilton says he was with his pal Robert Jensen,' Hamish said, 'so they're providing alibis for each other. Darius's cousin Stephen Palmerston was out in the snow wi' the other cousin, Henry Poulter. Alan Ferguson was wi' his brother, John. Who are the Ferguson brothers?'

'They're the ones from the band,' Priscilla said. 'They had come to find out if they could start setting up. They had an argument with Darius in reception.'

'Did they indeed?' Hamish said. 'That doesn't look good for them, does it? Who's on the final list you have there, Silas?'

'The prime suspects – people who have no one to vouch for them,' Silas said. 'A local lad – Donald Maclean – who was working here, the bridesmaid Helen Carter, Serena Hamilton, the groom Paul Hunter, Alannah Hamilton, Sebastian Chalmers, Viscount Carsely and . . . Priscilla.'

'Well, you can take me straight off that list!' Priscilla said, outraged. 'I am *not* a suspect – I am *not* a murderer!'

'Och, of course you're no',' Hamish said, calming her, 'and we can deal wi' that straight away. We'll have a wee chat and that'll make it official. There's one more to add to the prime suspects list – Sloane Beaumont.'

'That's even more ridiculous than having me on the list!' Priscilla objected. 'Poor Sloane's dead, for goodness' sake!'

'Aye, but we can't be sure when she died,' Hamish pointed out. 'There's a chance that she was killed after Darius Palmerston. Given that no one knew where she was, she might have murdered Darius. On the other hand, if she died before Palmerston, then he's a suspect in her murder, as is everyone else on our suspects list.'

'So where do we go from here?' Elspeth asked.

'We start looking for more evidence,' Hamish said, 'and I'll start interviewing the suspects, going over their initial statements to see if they can be ruled out. We can narrow the lists, starting wi' Priscilla.

'All right, here's what I need you to do. Silas, once the guests have had their breakfast, get them back to their rooms. You and Davey can then start taking a look at the phones o' those on our prime suspects list. We're looking for any suspicious photos or messages or voicemails. Elspeth, I want you to go through the video recordings you have. Again, we're looking for anything suspicious – anything that even looks a wee bit odd.'

'I'll get on to it straight away,' Elspeth said and she and Silas stood to leave.

'What about me?' Priscilla said. 'I need something to do. I can't bear just sitting around, waiting for the next disaster.'

'You'll have plenty to do when the team arrives from Strathbane later today,' Hamish said. 'In the meantime, bide here wi' me and we'll have that wee chat.'

'I don't think I can bear it if you start treating me like a criminal,' Priscilla said, casting a warning look at him.

'That's no' the way this is going to go,' Hamish said, smiling, opening a notebook and picking up his pen. 'We've known each other long enough for us to be able to run through all the standard stuff in just a few minutes. So, let's start wi' Darius. Where were you when he was killed?'

'I'd gone up to our private apartment,' she replied. 'All the stress of making sure that everything ran smoothly for the wedding had left me with a splitting headache so I went to take a painkiller and sat quietly in my room for a few minutes.'

'Did your parents see you up there?'

'No, my father was downstairs making a nuisance of himself with Mr Johnson and Mummy had gone to see Mrs Wellington, the minister's wife, about arranging for the flowers from the church to go to Braikie Hospital and one of the old folks' homes. She stayed there a while. She doesn't really like all the disturbance when the hotel is busy.'

'Okay,' Hamish said, making copious notes, 'but you were there quite quickly when the body was discovered.'

'Yes, I was on my way down the main staircase when I heard the screaming . . . I'll never forget that. Alannah looked like something out of a horror movie. I must check on her . . .'

'You knew Darius from down in London, of course,' Hamish said. 'Did you get on well wi' him?'

'I suppose so,' Priscilla said, drumming her fingers on the table. 'He was part of a group of friends. We got on well enough.'

Hamish looked down at her fingers, then back up into her eyes.

'I think you must have got on a wee bit better than that,' he said, setting aside his pen. 'So what was it wi' you and Darius?'

'At one time,' Priscilla answered, sitting back in her chair, 'I found him attractive. He was seen as quite a catch, you know. He was good looking, he could be very charming when he put his mind to it, and there were rumours about him having inherited a fortune.'

'You had an affair wi' him down in London, then?'

'We were together for a short while,' Priscilla said. That, Hamish mused, had always been the way with Priscilla. She had been engaged not only to him but to at least one other over the years and had enjoyed the attentions of a number of suitors, but her relationships had always fallen apart after 'a short while'.

'What made you break up wi' him?' Hamish knew he shouldn't really have asked, but he couldn't help himself. Had Palmerston suffered the same lack of affection, the same passionless lovemaking that had soured his own relationship with Priscilla? If so, he knew she would never admit that, but if she had any other answer for him, he wanted to know what it was.

'It became fairly obvious to me that he was seeing someone else,' Priscilla informed him. 'That would have been bad enough, of course, but it began to look like he wasn't what he liked people to think he was. I became very suspicious of him on all fronts, really, and decided he wasn't to be trusted.'

'Did you know who else he was seeing?'

'It could have been any number of girls who liked to be part of that set. There was a kind of party circuit and they would meet up in various clubs or restaurants.'

'Were Richard Wade and Simon Derringer part o' that set?'

'Yes, they appeared from time to time, but it was mainly me, Sloane, Helen, Alannah, Darius and, of course, Sebastian.'

'What made you think he was pulling the wool ower folks' eyes?'

'I was with him a couple of times when his credit card was refused in restaurants and I once heard him talking to Seb about gambling debts. Those two were always thick as thieves. Even when I was dating Darius, good old Sebastian was never far away. They shared a flat in Kensington, although I think they were kicked out of there. I once opened a sideboard drawer there that was stuffed full of unpaid bills and final demands.'

'Do you think he was broke?'

'I'm certain of it. He was always scrounging cash from me. He used to say it was "just until I can sort out a problem with the bank in Geneva". That always sounded dodgy, even if only because the major banking centre in Switzerland is Zurich. If he was as rich as he always said, that's where he'd have his bank.'

'Did you give him money?'

'You should know better than to ask that!' Priscilla laughed. 'I never gave him more cash than he needed to buy us a couple of drinks in a bar. I know you've never been interested in money, Hamish, but you know I keep a close eye on the finances here at the hotel. I don't ever again want to end up in the situation Daddy got us into. Ultimately, that was why I ditched Darius. I couldn't trust him and I became convinced that all he wanted was money. He was only interested in me because he thought it might be a way for him to get his hands on all of this.' She waved a hand around her to indicate the hotel. 'I hated him for that.'

'Do you think Alannah was the one he was cheating on you wi'?'

'No,' Priscilla said. 'He used to flirt with her when he was supposed to be with me, but he flirted with almost any woman. It was months after I finished with him that they became a couple.'

'Did you no' warn her what he was like?'

'Of course,' Priscilla said. 'She asked me if I would be upset if she started dating him and I told her she was welcome to him, but that she should actually stay well clear of him. I warned her he was trouble and that he was only after her money.'

'Do you no' mean her father's money?'

'No, Hamish. All of Alannah's friends know that she will inherit an absolute fortune when she gets married. It's something to do with a trust set up for her by her grandfather. I've no doubt whatsoever that's why Darius went after her. Once you got to know him, you could see what a liar and schemer he was, wheedling his way into your confidence so he could take advantage of you. That's why I hated him so much.'

'Now you've said that,' Hamish pointed out, 'you must realise that I'm wondering if you hated him enough to kill him.'

'I know you've got your policeman's head on, Hamish,'

she said, 'but do be serious. I was no longer enamoured of Darius Palmerston and yes, I hated him for the way he tried to use me, but I'm not stupid enough to want to kill him. I'm certainly not stupid enough to arrange his wedding here in *my* hotel in order to kill him on his wedding day.'

'After all you've told me, I'm a wee bit surprised that you agreed to have the wedding here at all.'

'When we all heard the announcement that Alannah and Darius were engaged, there was a lot of talk about weddings. I told Helen that we often hosted weddings at Tommel Castle and she thought it was a wonderfully romantic setting. She then talked to Alannah, who asked me if I could arrange for the wedding to be here. I wasn't about to turn down the sort of profit that the Hamiltons would bring. In a way, that was payback for the way Darius had behaved.'

'Did you ever find out who Darius was two-timing you wi'?'

'No, but it was a long time ago. Ancient history now – uncomfortable memories.'

'Was it why you decided to start spending so much more time up here, away from London?'

'I don't think that's really got anything to do with Darius's murder,' Priscilla said, standing and smoothing her skirt. 'I think we're finished here, Hamish, don't you?'

'Aye, unless there's anything more you have to say.'

'Actually, there is one thing,' Priscilla said, frowning slightly while making an effort to remember correctly. 'You should ask Mr Johnson about the band. I think he saw what happened when Darius argued with Alan Ferguson. By the time I got here everything had calmed down a bit but Ferguson was very unhappy with Darius.'

'Wi' any luck, we'll have that on the security camera,' Hamish said, then looked up as Davey burst into the room.

'Hamish, you'd better come and take a look outside,' he said breathlessly. 'I went to check on Paul Hunter, and he's gone!'

'How can he have gone?' Hamish said. 'Where the hell can he go? He can't get out o' the village!'

'He can,' Davey assured him. 'Maybe he couldn't get out of here by car, but he's taken one of the horses and there are tracks leading up towards the path we walked on Friday. I think he's heading for the Spaniard's Leap!'

'The bloody fool!' Hamish groaned, rushing out of the room with Davey. 'He's liable to kill himself up there!'

'There's more,' Davey said as they dashed down the hotel steps. Hamish paused at the foot of the steps.

'What do you mean, more?'

'I took a look in his bedsit and found the grey waistcoat and trousers he was wearing yesterday. They're covered in blood!'

Chapter Seven

Fortunately for mankind the brain in a life of action turns more to the matter in hand than to conjuring up the chances of the future.
　　　　　　　　　　John Buchan, Prester John (1910)

Hamish and Davey ran round the hotel to the stable block, their boots crunching on the fresh snow. They stopped when they reached the horses' stalls. The door to Blaze's stall stood open, the snow outside had been trampled and Blaze was gone. Brandy looked out from his with a forlorn expression, dismayed at having been left behind when his friend was ridden away.

'How long since Hunter left?' Hamish asked, turning to Davey.

'I doubt he'd have gone while it was still snowing,' Davey reasoned. 'Visibility would have been zilch up on the hillside.'

'Aye,' Hamish agreed. 'Nor would he have gone while it was dark for the same reason. So he waited until the snow stopped, and as soon as he had good daylight, he took his chance. I'd say he's been gone no more than forty minutes.'

Pulling on latex gloves, they went into the bedsit and Davey showed Hamish where he'd found the bloodied clothes stuffed into the bottom of the wardrobe beneath a blanket.

'The blood's all smeared,' Hamish said, studying the waistcoat. 'There are no spatter marks at all.'

'Maybe he tried to wipe it off,' Davey suggested.

'Aye, maybe,' Hamish said, thinking hard. 'Let's get back to the incident room and work out how we handle this.'

Back in the hotel, Hamish called Silas, Priscilla and Elspeth into the incident room and spread a map out on the table.

'The tracks out by the stables show that Paul Hunter took one o' the horses and headed off this way,' he said. 'He's following the route we took wi' the walking group up to the Spaniard's Leap, but that's the scenic ramble. There's a more direct route that cuts across the foot o' Ben Diabhail here.' He indicated the alternative path. 'He's got too much o' a head start for us to cut him off, but we might be able to catch him up, especially on horseback.'

'I'll go after him,' Alannah Hamilton volunteered from the doorway. Her face was pale and she appeared smaller than she had looked before the wedding, as though all of the trauma had somehow managed to shrink her. Compared to the confident, self-assured young woman who had watched auld Angus issue his dire warnings, Hamish thought, she looked quite frail.

'He's taken Blaze, hasn't he?' she said. 'That's his favourite. I can go after him on Brandy. I can catch him up and persuade him to come back.'

'He's surely not planning to take the leap on horseback, is he?' Silas asked.

'No – Paul won't do that. He won't do anything that puts Blaze in danger. He . . . he loves those horses . . .'

Alannah glanced down at the carpet then raised her chin, engaging each of the others in turn with a look of proud defiance. 'Whatever you think Paul's done, you're wrong. You don't know him like I do. He could never have done that to Darius. Paul is not a murderer and if you give us a chance, we'll prove it. I'll go after him and bring him back.'

'I'm sorry, lass,' Hamish said, 'but I can't allow you to do that. I wouldn't be doing my job if I let you go out there.'

'I'll go,' Davey said. 'Freddy said we could put Mr Chalmers in his room as he'll be in the kitchen all day. One of the other constables is looking after him. That means I can go after Paul. Miss . . .' he almost called her Miss Hamilton, but caught himself in time, '. . . if you would come out with me to saddle up Brandy, that might help him to get to know me a little better. I'm a good rider, and I'll look after him. I know the route. It's an easy, wide path through the trees most of the way. I walked it with Susan in the summer.'

'That's settled then,' Hamish said, looking back at the map to point out a road. 'This small road follows the other side o' the Anstey up to a layby and picnic spot on the far side o' the Spaniard's Leap. I'll take the Land Rover up there and cover the other side o' the gorge.'

'But the road will still be blocked,' Priscilla pointed out. 'The snow may have stopped but the only roads anyone will even be thinking about clearing are the main routes. That one will be deep with snow.'

'No, yon wee road will be clear,' Hamish said, grinning. 'My cousin Callum's farm is on that road and he'll have kept the snow at bay so he can get out to earn the council's hourly snow-clearing rate on the big roads.'

Hamish left Priscilla and Silas to ensure that all the guests returned to their rooms once they'd had breakfast and that Jimmy's constables maintained their guard rota. He asked Elspeth to come with him in the Land Rover.

'If we need to try talking him into heading away from the ledge,' he explained, 'you might have a gentler voice for persuading him. It might also be handy to have you in the car in any case.'

Minutes later, Davey was in the saddle, wearing a pair of flat-soled boots borrowed from Freddy. His own work boots wouldn't have fitted Brandy's stirrups. Alannah had spread a concoction on Brandy's hooves to stop balls of frozen snow forming and the horse was raring to go, keen to get out and find his stablemate.

Although the snow had stopped, the sky was still thick with cloud and it was cold, both his breath and Brandy's forming misty plumes of condensation. Once they picked up the path through the forest, they also picked up their pace, Brandy happy to trot and Davey happy that his rusty riding technique was up to the task.

He was enjoying riding through the snow, among the trees, in the fresh mountain air so much that he imagined himself as a Wild West lawman on the trail of some bank robber or bandit who'd held up the stagecoach. He shook his head and scolded himself. He wasn't a sheriff in the old west, he was a Scottish police constable. This was a serious business and he needed to concentrate.

When he broke out of the trees, the snow-covered slope stretched ahead of him, dotted with boulders that had somehow shrugged off the snowflakes. The path was easy to follow, climbing across the slope that fell away to the left and sweeping round giant buttresses of rock rising to the right. He could also now see the tracks Blaze had left in the snow and, on rounding one outcrop, he spotted the small figures of the horse and its rider in the distance further up the mountain. Brandy either saw or scented them, too, quickening his pace to try to catch up. Davey reined him in, wary that a slip or stumble could prove disastrous.

Paul appeared to be concentrating on the route ahead, never looking back and so never realising that Davey was gaining on him. He had a hat pulled down over his ears and was clearly unable to hear Brandy above the whistle of the light wind and the noise Blaze was making pounding through the snow. Davey watched him approach the final bend before the Spaniard's Leap, where Paul dismounted at a small stand of stalwart pine trees that had managed to establish themselves in the shelter of some rocks despite the ravages of the wind and the appetites of the deer. He tied Blaze's reins to a tree branch, only then looking back to see Davey less than two hundred metres down the trail.

Davey cursed when Paul quickly pushed through the knee-deep snow to disappear round the bend. He let Brandy trot on faster, then eased himself out of the saddle when they reached Blaze. He tethered Brandy to a tree and followed the lines Paul had cut when he kicked his way through the snow. He found him sitting on a rock, staring out across the gorge.

'Paul,' he said gently. 'It's me, Davey.'

'Don't come any closer,' Paul said without looking round. 'I wondered who they would send after me. I thought it might be Sergeant Macbeth in a mountain rescue helicopter or something. I didn't think it would be you riding Brandy.'

'It nearly wasn't me,' Davey said. 'Alannah wanted to come. She's worried about you, Paul.'

'They wouldn't let me see her.' Paul put his face in his hands. 'After all that horror she went through, they wouldn't even let me be in the same room with her – wouldn't even tell me how she was.'

'I can tell you. She's doing okay, Paul. She's strong and smart and she's going to be fine.'

'Well, she'll definitely be better off without me around.'

He snatched some snow from the ground and hurled it into the gorge.

'That's not the way she sees it. She's ready to fight for you. She wants you back so she can prove you're innocent. She knows you didn't kill Darius or Sloane.'

'Sloane?' Paul jumped to his feet. 'What's happened to Sloane? No ... the bastards have done for her, too, haven't they? Why her? She was fun. What harm did she ever do anyone? They'll pin that on me, too! They'll make me their scapegoat. They'll blame me for everything!'

'Calm down, Paul. Who are "they"?'

'Them – the Hamiltons, Jensen, Wade, Derringer – the whole bunch of filthy, money-grabbing pigs!'

'Paul, if you know anything about what happened yesterday, then we need you to share it with us. We need you to come back down to the hotel so we can sort out this whole mess.'

'I think I'd rather take my chances here,' Paul said, taking a couple of steps closer to the edge of the gorge. 'It doesn't look that far and I bet I'm fitter than that old Spanish sailor. I'm not weighed down with pockets full of gold, either.'

Davey moved a little closer to Paul. He could now hear the torrent crashing over the rocks deep in the gorge although the sound, like all others on the mountain, was softly muted, absorbed by the snow. He was desperately trying to work out whether he could rush out and grab Paul before he could attempt the jump.

'Bide where you are now, Paul,' Hamish's voice drifted across the gorge, 'and listen very carefully. I can't shout because you've walked out past the rock ledge – you're now standing right out on the snow cornice. Even the sound o' my voice could send vibrations through it that'll make it break away.'

Paul stayed still as a statue, staring across at Hamish, who was standing on the other side of the leap in the snow, the high-vis Police Scotland jacket he was wearing making him almost luminous against the dark trees behind him, the brightest object anywhere in sight.

'Very slowly, take a step back,' Hamish said. 'No sudden moves now – just take it easy.'

Paul did as he was told and there came a low rumbling noise followed by the hiss of ice crystals tumbling down the cliff face into the gorge.

'The cornice is going, Paul!' Hamish shouted. 'Jump now, man! Jump!'

Paul launched himself through the air across the Spaniard's Leap but the cornice collapsed beneath him, robbing him of half the power his legs put into the take-off. Davey watched him reaching out towards Hamish as though it were all happening in slow motion. Hamish also reached out his arms but it was abundantly clear that Paul wasn't going to make it. Then, to his astonishment, Davey saw Hamish jump, connecting with Paul in midair and wrapping his arms and legs around him. A heartbeat later, both men had disappeared into the gorge.

Scarcely able to believe what he had just witnessed, Davey dropped to his knees, horrified, and crawled forward as far as he dared to peer over the edge. Then he heard the crackle of a police radio.

'All right, Elspeth, bring us up!'

Hamish was dangling just two metres down, supported in a high-vis harness that was indiscernible from his jacket. Attached to the harness was a cable, most of which had sunk into the snow on the other side of the gorge. Davey could make out the whine of the Land Rover's winch from somewhere beyond the trees. Paul was clinging to Hamish and Hamish to Paul as they inched upwards to the lip of the gorge.

When they reached the edge, Paul scrambled clear of Hamish into the snow and, with Hamish still being dragged upwards, he attempted to make a run for it. Instead, he fell flat on his face.

'That's no' very grateful, now, is it?' Hamish said, crawling into the snow and holding up his wrist, which he had handcuffed to Paul's ankle. The radio crackled again. 'That's far enough, Elspeth.'

Davey sat back in the snow, catching his breath and watching Hamish reposition the handcuffs, slapping them on Paul's wrists.

'Hamish Macbeth!' he yelled, rolling a handful of snow and hurling it across the Spaniard's Leap at his sergeant. It disintegrated on Hamish's shoulder. 'Don't ever do that to me again!'

'You get those two bonny horses back to Tommel Castle,' Hamish called, grinning at Davey, 'afore I arrest you for assaulting a superior officer wi' a snowball!'

*

Hamish was sitting in the incident room with Paul, steaming mugs of coffee in front of them, when Davey arrived back. Paul was still in handcuffs.

'That was some stunt you pulled back there,' Davey said to Hamish, still with a note of anger in his voice. 'Let me know next time you try something stupid like that – I don't want to see you kill yourself!'

'Och, it wasn't as bad as all that,' Hamish said, slightly peeved that his constable should be taking that tone with him. 'Paul was the one in real danger. I came away wi' just a bruised shoulder, although the straps on yon mountain rescue harness didn't half tighten around my groin. Truth be told, I'm still feeling a wee bit uncomfortable in the trouser department.'

He gave Davey the same wide grin he'd flashed at him across the Spaniard's Leap and the constable dropped himself into a chair, sighing and smiling.

'I guess that's what I get for agreeing to work with Hamish Macbeth,' he said.

'You guess right, Constable Forbes. Now,' he said, opening a notebook and picking up a pen. 'Let's have a wee chat, Paul. I want the truth from you, mind – you owe me at least that for saving your life.'

'You can have the truth,' Paul answered, 'but you might not believe it.'

'Where were you when Darius Palmerston was murdered?' Hamish asked.

'I was out at the stables, tending to Blaze and Brandy,' Paul answered.

'So – why did you take it into your head to run off to the Spaniard's Leap this morning?'

'Because it's the only way out of the village right now,' Paul replied.

'Quite so,' Hamish said, 'but why did you feel the need to escape from Lochdubh?'

'You know why,' Paul said. 'You must have found that bloodstained uniform in my wardrobe.'

'That we did. Are you saying that you thought we'd believe those clothes proved you to be the killer of Darius Palmerston and Sloane Beaumont?'

'I didn't know anything about Sloane having been killed. I really liked her. She was always laughing and joking, always teasing. I can't believe she's gone.'

'Did you murder Sloane Beaumont?' Hamish asked.

'No, of course I didn't,' Paul said, 'and I didn't kill Darius, either. I'm not a killer, Sergeant Macbeth, no matter how it might look.'

'So how did your clothes get covered in blood, Paul?' Davey asked.

'I've no idea. They were fine when I hung them in that wardrobe but when I went to take a shirt out, the waistcoat and trousers weren't there. I thought they might have fallen off the hanger, then found them under a blanket at the bottom of the wardrobe.'

'Do you expect us to believe that someone else sneaked into your bedsit, smeared your clothes wi' blood and left them to be found in order to implicate you in the murders?' asked Hamish.

'No, I definitely didn't expect you'd believe that,' Paul explained. 'That's why I ran away. It was crystal clear to me that someone was trying to frame me for Darius's murder.'

'How well did you get on with Darius?' Davey chimed in.

'I didn't get on with him at all. I hated him. He was a liar, a cheat and a fraud – the worst scumbag ever to walk the earth.'

'Not your favourite person, then,' Hamish said, 'and hate is a powerful motive for murder.'

'I didn't kill him. I won't pretend I'm not glad that he's dead, but I didn't kill him. I couldn't do something like that, and I had no real reason to do it, anyway.'

'In my experience,' Hamish said, setting his pen aside and sitting back in his chair, 'anyone can turn into a killer under the right circumstances, and maybe you did have a reason.'

'What do you mean?' Paul shifted warily.

'How did you get on wi' the Hamiltons?' Hamish asked.

'They're good employers,' Paul responded. 'I love my job.'

'Aye, but that's no' what I asked,' Hamish said, leaning his elbows on the table. 'Up on the mountain you described them as "filthy money-grabbing pigs".'

'Charles and Serena are only interested in money,' Paul said.

'But not Alannah?' Davey asked. 'Is she different? What sort of relationship do you have with her?'

'She *is* different,' Paul said, then looked down at his handcuffs. 'She treats me as an equal. We both love the horses and go riding together. She's more like . . . a friend.'

'Paul,' Hamish said, shaking his head, 'you said you'd be truthful wi' us and that was a blatant lie. Alannah's no' just a friend, is she?'

Paul stared across the table at Hamish with a look of a man who realises the game he's playing is running towards full time and any chance of victory is ebbing away. Hamish placed two evidence bags containing Paul and Alannah's phones on the table.

'Look at it from our point of view, Paul,' Davey suggested. 'We've seen the messages you and Alannah exchanged. We know you're having an affair. I'd go so far as to say the two of you are in love. That gives you a pretty powerful incentive to want Darius out of the way.'

'Love and hate,' Hamish pointed out, 'are the two most deadly emotions.'

'You're right,' Paul said. 'I love Alannah more than I can say, and I've already told you how much I hated Darius. He treated her so badly.'

'In what way?' Davey asked.

'In every way,' Paul said. 'He was never faithful to her. I think she was quite charmed by him in the beginning, but that really didn't last long. He was always with other women. Even when they got engaged, I'd see him when we were at equestrian events hitting on other women – usually older, always stinking rich. Alannah felt totally humiliated.'

'Why did she put up wi' that?' Hamish asked.

'I don't really want to talk about—' Paul began but was interrupted when Alannah burst into the room.

'I'm sorry, Hamish,' Silas said, chasing right behind her. 'She slipped right past me.'

'Paul!' Alannah sobbed, tears in her eyes. She threw her arms around him, then looked down at his wrists. 'Handcuffs? No . . . not handcuffs! You can't do this to him! He hasn't done anything. He's innocent!'

Paul looked stunned, whispering her name as Hamish pulled them apart.

'That remains to be seen, lass,' he said calmly, easing the couple apart, 'but in the meantime I can't let you two see each other.'

Silas escorted a tearful Alannah out of the room and Hamish talked quietly to Paul.

'No doubt we'll have to have another wee chat,' Hamish said, 'but there's others I'd like to talk to first. In the meantime, the safest place for you is the cell in my police station. Davey, take him away.'

The colonel marched into the room the moment Davey and Paul had left.

'Got your man, eh, Macbeth?' he said, rubbing his hands in delight. 'Jolly good show. Maybe now we can get back to normal before the guests go stir crazy. Charles Hamilton just wants to get his wife and daughter out of here.'

'I'm sure he does,' Hamish said, 'but that'll no' be happening just yet. We have a person who has submitted himself to my custody, but this investigation is far from ower. The guests must stay in their rooms for now and I'll tell that to Mr Hamilton myself. I'd like him to come down for a talk wi' me anyway.'

The colonel's shoulders dropped and he shuffled out of the room, muttering that he'd let Charles Hamilton know. Barely had he departed than Elspeth knocked on the door.

'Sorry if I'm interrupting anything,' she said, hovering in the doorway, 'but I've a couple of things to show you.'

'Come away in,' Hamish said, waving her forward. 'You're no' interrupting. If an incident room's no' busy, then there's nothing happening.'

'I've raced through a lot of the video I recorded yesterday,' she explained, setting up a laptop on the table. 'This is what I've come up with so far. The first clip was taken immediately after the speeches, when Charles Hamilton and my boss were out on the terrace smoking cigars.'

'That would be immediately before Palmerston was murdered,' Hamish said.

'Exactly,' Elspeth agreed. 'I left the camera sitting on its tripod while I was talking to the other guests. Jensen had told me to keep it running, so I hadn't switched it off. You can't hear much of what Hamilton and Jensen are saying, but I've got some software on here that helped me to isolate and enhance some of it.'

The clip showed Hamilton and Jensen standing outside with their backs to the dining-room French windows. They were smoking large cigars and had been the only ones brave or foolish enough to venture out into the snow.

'We can't let him carry on the way he is,' Hamish heard Jensen say through a rustle of static. 'He'll ruin us! You have to get rid of him! He has to be terminated!'

'I'll deal with him,' Hamilton replied. 'Seems a shame to be doing that on the wedding day, though, Robert.'

'Sooner rather than later would be best,' Jensen replied, then both men walked off along the terrace, out of shot.

'Looks like they had it in for somebody,' Hamish said. 'They didn't actually mention Palmerston, but that didn't sound good.'

'Here's the other clip.' Elspeth opened another file on the laptop. 'It was just after everyone arrived at the hotel from the church. Again, the camera was sitting on its tripod. I was at the bar getting a champagne refill. Darius and Sebastian clearly didn't realise the camera was running when they chose a quiet spot right next to it for a little heart-to-heart.'

The two men could be seen on screen walking away from everyone else in the bar area. Darius had his arm around his best man's shoulders and Sebastian looked like he was weeping. They stopped close to the camera where their faces were out of shot, although parts of their jackets and kilts filled the screen. There was a great deal of background chatter, but their voices could be heard crisp and clear.

'Don't worry, Seb,' Darius said. 'Everything's going to work out. We're sitting pretty now and I'll take care of you. I always have done, haven't I? Everything's going to be fine – just like always.'

'But it's not fine, is it? It's not like always!' Sebastian's voice wavered with emotion but still managed to convey an undercurrent of rage. 'You're married now. That changes everything. Where does it leave me?'

'Keep your cool, mate,' Darius advised. 'Don't lose your head and I promise we'll come out of this smelling of roses.'

The two then walked away from the camera and whatever else they might have said was lost in the dozens of other conversations swirling round the room. Elspeth closed the laptop.

'Your best friend – your best man – is usually happy for you when you get married,' Hamish said, running a hand through his hair and frowning. 'What was Chalmers so upset about? Palmerston clearly had some plot hatching that he thought would see them both right.'

'Whatever he was planning went disastrously wrong,' Elspeth said. 'That's all I've got for now, but I'll keep looking. Jensen is still badgering me about filing a story.'

'Aye, I'm sure he is,' Hamish replied, 'but if you could keep it quiet for now, at least until the team arrives later today, I'd be grateful. Dealing wi' the press is something I can do without.'

When Elspeth opened the door to leave, Charles Hamilton strode over from the reception area, where Silas had intercepted him.

'I was told you wanted to see me,' Hamilton said to Hamish.

'Aye, that's right, Mr Hamilton,' Hamish said, inviting him in. 'Would you like a coffee? I'm about ready for another one myself.'

Having heard Hamish, Silas nodded and headed to the bar, while Hamilton seated himself, placing an iPad squarely on the table in front of him.

'I understand you have someone in custody for the murder of my son-in-law,' Hamilton stated.

'We have a person who is helping us with our enquiries,' Hamish said.

'And that person is Paul Hunter, is it not?' Hamilton's question was, once again, more of a statement of fact.

'I don't think that's much o' a secret,' Hamish said.

'Then I'd like to leave with my family as soon as possible,' said Hamilton, 'but I have a little problem.' He held up his iPad. 'Since you have confiscated our phones – and you can be sure I'll be complaining about that to your superiors in the strongest possible terms – Robert and I contacted our people by email to summon the helicopter only to be told that Lochdubh has been designated a "no-fly zone" due to an ongoing police incident.'

'Really?' Hamish said with a shrug. 'I ken nothing about that, Mr Hamilton. That would be way above my pay grade, as they say. I can let my superiors know that you're anxious to be on your way.

'Good,' Hamilton said, breathing in and closing his eyes. He patted his chest with his right hand. 'The stress of the wedding was bad enough, but with everything else on top, it's enough to give me another heart attack.'

They fell silent when Silas arrived with their coffee.

'What I really wanted to ask you about,' Hamish said as Silas left the room again, 'were the arrangements surrounding the wedding yesterday.'

'What arrangements do you mean?'

'It's my understanding that Alannah was to receive some kind of inheritance when she married.'

'That's correct,' Hamilton confirmed. 'It was a trust fund set up by my father. She now has access to the entire fund. I pressed a button as soon as she was legally wed and my people made sure that she became a very wealthy woman.'

'How wealthy?'

'She's now worth many, many times more than you will earn in your entire life.'

'Would Darius Palmerston have had access to that money?'

'Not a penny. He signed an agreement that left him entitled to precisely none of it. In fact, nobody has access to it except Alannah – not even me. Of course, I expect she will invest wisely through the family business and I will help her do that, but she controls that money, no one else. Palmerston certainly wasn't going to get his hands on it.'

'It doesn't sound like you trusted him very much.'

'I didn't trust him at all,' Hamilton said, sitting back and crossing his legs. 'I know exactly what he was like. You don't think I would let my only child marry some chap I knew nothing about, do you? It took just a few phone calls for my people to find out that he had run up debts all over Europe, mainly in the south of France.

Hotels, restaurants, casinos, you name it – and I've no doubt he fleeced a few wealthy widows along the way, too. He was a complete scoundrel.'

'Why would you let a man like that marry your daughter?'

'Because she wanted to, Sergeant. She said it would make her happy and, in the end, I knew she would go ahead and do whatever she wanted, whether she had my blessing or not. That's what Alannah's like. I can't control her but, ultimately, I knew I could control him. We came to an agreement – I would take care of the debts that were chasing him around Europe and he would come to work for me.'

'You were prepared to let someone like that loose on your clients' investments?'

'Good God, no!' Hamilton burst out laughing. 'We'd have found him something in PR or client liaison where he was kept well away from access to anything to do with money. He might actually have been an asset in that sort of role. The only things he had going for him were that he looked presentable, he had the gift of the gab and he could be utterly charming – when he wasn't being a complete arse. The best way for me to keep control of my whole family and protect the business was to bring him inside where I could keep a proper eye on him.'

'Thank you for being so frank wi' me, Mr Hamilton. You've been very helpful,' Hamish said, and then paused, flicking through his notebook. 'One last thing. You told one o' the constables that you were outside on the terrace when Darius was killed. You were having a cigar and a chat wi' Mr Jensen.'

'That's right.'

'What were you chatting about?'

'Now you mention it,' Hamilton said, stroking his nose as though deep in thought, 'I can't really remember. Shouldn't think it was anything important.'

Hamish showed Hamilton out, handing him back to Silas who was waiting to escort him safely back to his room. He also asked Silas to bring Robert Jensen to the incident room, then returned to sit at the table. Hamilton had lied about his conversation with Jensen. Stroking his nose would have been a dead giveaway, even if Hamish hadn't already seen and heard Elspeth's recording. Nobody forgets talking about getting rid of someone or being told to 'terminate him'. The question was, were they talking about Palmerston and, if not, why had he lied?

He was still mulling it over when Jensen walked in. He was carrying an iPad just like Hamilton's and, just as Hamilton had done, he set it neatly on the table in front of him when he took his seat. Unlike Hamilton, he had the whisper of a smile playing on his lips. Hamish thanked him for coming and made a show of flicking through his notebook while he wondered what the hell Jensen found so amusing.

'Mr Jensen, I really have only one question for you,' he said, thinking to himself, *apart from why don't you wipe yon stupid smile off your face?*

'Good, then we can keep this brief,' Jensen replied.

'What I want to ask,' Hamish continued, 'is what were you and Mr Hamilton talking about on the terrace after the speeches?'

Jensen's smile collapsed and he gave Hamish a sharp look.

'None of your business,' he said.

'A man has been murdered,' Hamish pointed out.

'That makes everything surrounding that fateful moment very much my business.'

'It had nothing to do with the murder,' Jensen asserted. 'Nothing for you to get all suspicious about.'

'I'll be the judge o' that,' Hamish asserted, 'and I think you telling Charles Hamilton that a man "has to be terminated" and asking him to "get rid of him" is very suspicious indeed.'

'Oh, do you?' Jensen's smile flicked back on. 'Well, I don't know where you got all that from – I very much doubt it was from Charles – but it's still none of your business.'

'I had one question for you, Mr Jensen,' Hamish said, sounding as sternly officious as he could to bolster the lie he was presenting, 'and you have failed to answer it to my satisfaction. I'm of a mind, therefore, to take you into custody at Lochdubh police station for further questioning.'

Quite how he might lock Jensen up when Paul was occupying his only cell, Hamish neglected to explain. His lie would have been blown out of the water had Jensen any idea of the limited facilities available.

'You're serious, aren't you?' Jensen gasped, incredulous. 'Even though I'm already as good as a prisoner here?'

'There's no' the same level o' creature comforts at the station, I'm afraid,' Hamish said, backing up his lie with an absolute truth, 'and I'd have to take that thing off you.' He pointed to Jensen's iPad.

'Ah, yes,' Jensen said, with a small chuckle, tapping the iPad. 'I've something to show you on here. Tell you what, I'll answer your question, then show you what's on here, if you then answer a question for me.'

Hamish nodded.

'Through his company, Hamilton Investments, and using his clients' money, Charles is a major investor in my outfit, Jensen Media,' Jensen explained. 'I should also point out that I, and my employees' pension fund, invest a great deal of money through Hamilton Investments. It's a mutually beneficial arrangement, and a matter of public record.

'Unfortunately, it has come to light that one of Charles's people has been ripping us both off to line his own pockets. He's the one that we had to "get rid of". Charles, however, is incredibly scandal shy. He's always out to protect the family name and, hence, the business. I can't criticise him for that because it's a policy that has worked well and kept his family's wealth intact. I, on the other hand, thrive on scandal.'

He opened the iPad and flicked through a few online news headlines. The least scurrilous was HIGHLAND WEDDING MURDER but the less subtle ran along the lines of BLOODSTAINED BRIDE'S HUSBAND BUTCHERED and WED AND DEAD. Hamish closed his eyes and let out a groan of misery and disdain.

'You can't shut down a free press, Sergeant,' Jensen told him gleefully. 'You took our phones and locked us up in this hotel. You even stopped our helicopter coming in, all to try to bury this story, but that's simply not possible. The staff working here went home and talked to their families who immediately got on their phones to gossip with friends and relatives far and wide. A story like this always gets out. Charles knows that. He hates being part of a bad news story, but the only way to deal with that is to be in control of it. You were not in control, but I was. I emailed my office and gave them the story straight from me, right here on the scene. They've syndicated it across every outlet in the country.

'Now the whole thing's about to go global, so I have my one question for you, Sergeant Hamish Macbeth – where is Sloane Beaumont?'

'None o' your business,' Hamish replied, repeating Jensen's previous mantra. 'You can go now.'

Hamish directed Jensen back into the care of Silas in reception, then turned to be confronted by the most unlikely visitors to the Tommel Castle Hotel – Nessie and Jessie Currie.

'It is Sunday. We have just come from the kirk service,' Nessie said, 'and noticed that you were not there – as usual.'

'As usual,' repeated Jessie.

'Aye, well I've been a wee bit busy here,' Hamish said, 'and I still am, so I need to—'

'We have important information,' Nessie interrupted, 'which you will want to hear.'

'*Will* want to hear,' echoed Jessie, nodding emphatically.

'Okay, ladies,' Hamish said, standing with his arms folded, 'let's hear it.'

And the Currie twins said in complete unison:

'We know who murdered Darius Palmerston!'

Chapter Eight

The rank is but the guinea's stamp,
The Man's the gowd for a' that.
   Robert Burns, 'A Man's a Man for a' That' (1795)

Hamish settled the Currie twins at the table in the incident room, offering them coffee.

'Thank you, Sergeant Macbeth, but we don't drink coffee,' Nessie informed him.

'Don't drink coffee,' Jessie confirmed.

'One cup and we'd be wide awake until Wednesday,' Nessie explained.

'Awake until Wednesday,' chorused Jessie.

'We will wait until we get home. After kirk on Sunday we always have a nice cup of tea in the living room and a slice of our homemade shortbread.'

'Homemade shortbread.'

'Sounds braw,' Hamish said, having enjoyed the Curries' shortbread many times in the past when they had dropped some off at the police station as a gift. 'There's nothing comes close to your homemade shortie. Now, what is it you wanted to tell me . . . No, let's start at the beginning. How did you ken there had been a murder?'

'It's all over the village,' Nessie said. 'Everyone knows

the bridegroom at the posh wedding was killed at the reception with his own sword that was used to cut the cake.'

'Cut the cake,' came Jessie's echo.

'It's also been reported on the line-net-interweb,' Nessie said, not quite understanding the terminology but repeating what she had been told.

'Line-net-interweb,' Jessie said, nodding her agreement, but equally in the dark.

'Aye, I suppose half the world kens by now,' Hamish said. 'So what makes you think you ken who did it?'

'We heard him say he was going to do it,' Nessie claimed. 'We heard him say he would "kill the . . ."'

'Kill the bastard!' When her sister showed but a moment's hesitation, Jessie took her chance to finish the sentence with relish.

'Who did you hear saying that?' Hamish asked.

'The nephew of that smelly old fisherman, Archie Maclean,' Nessie said. 'Always smoking and always in the pub.'

'Always in the pub.'

'That's where they were going when they stopped outside our cottage on Friday night,' said Nessie. 'We were in our dressing gowns ready for bed. Fortunately, we had already drawn the curtains.'

'Drawn the curtains.'

'We peeked out when we heard voices and we then heard Archie and Donald Maclean deciding not to go to the pub. They saw Mr Palmerston heading there and Donald Maclean sounded very bitter about Mr Palmerston "winding him up". He said if Mr Palmerston did it one more time, he would—'

'Kill the bastard!' Jessie's enthusiasm got the better of

her and she jumped in a little too early, cutting her sister off, drawing a disapproving scowl from Nessie.

'Well, thank you, ladies, I'm sure that's going to be very useful,' Hamish said, thinking he was drawing the conversation to a close, but the Currie twins showed no inclination to move. He was wondering what might be the most diplomatic way to get them out of his incident room when Davey walked in.

'Sergeant Macbeth,' he said, using a serious, official tone that was clearly intended for the twins, 'there's something urgent I need to show you in the office.'

'I'll be right wi' you, Constable Forbes,' Hamish said and apologised to Nessie and Jessie for having to 'get on wi' police business'. Having removed neither their hats nor their coats and even having kept their hands fully gloved, the twins got up and walked at a briskly synchronised pace out into the snow.

'I really do have something for you to see, Hamish,' Davey said, leading the way to Mr Johnson's office. Mr Johnson then played them a recording from the reception area camera the previous day. Unlike Elspeth's recordings, there was no sound.

'That's yon lads in the band arriving,' Hamish said. 'Priscilla said there had been some sort o' stramash.'

They watched as Darius appeared and stopped in front of the five men, pointing to the door and apparently telling them to leave. There was a brief argument and a scuffle broke out between Darius and one of the Ferguson brothers. The other brother then pushed his way between them to put a stop to it.

'It's hard to tell, but I think Darius just threw a punch,' Davey said.

'Aye, and I'd say he landed it as well,' Hamish agreed.

'The band's staying at Mrs Mackenzie's place, Davey. Find the Ferguson brothers and bring them in. Once you've done that, you can pick up Donald Maclean. I'm wanting a wee word wi' him, too.'

'Will do,' Davey said, pulling on a pair of latex gloves. 'Take a look at this first, though.'

He fished a phone out of an evidence bag and called up a text message.

'Silas and I started looking at these early this morning and came across this on Chalmers's phone. It's a message from him to Darius.'

The message simply read: **SHE KNOWS**

They walked back to the incident room together, Hamish watching as Davey scrolled through other messages.

'When was that message sent?' Hamish asked.

'On the morning of the wedding,' Davey answered. 'I checked Darius's phone and he read the message but didn't reply.'

'Why is the best man sending cryptic messages like that to the groom on his wedding day?' Hamish wondered out loud. 'Who might "she" be and what is it that she knows?'

'Exactly,' Davey said, 'but there are no messages at all after that on either phone and none before that give us any sort of clue as to who "she" might be.'

'Well done, Davey,' Hamish said. 'Now you go and bring in the Fergusons. I need to give Jimmy a quick call.'

Jimmy was wide awake and raring to go when Hamish got through to him.

'My team is getting together now, Hamish,' he said. 'The snowploughs are at work and we'll be wi' you by nightfall.'

'You can't get here soon enough for me, Jimmy,' Hamish said. 'The press have got their teeth into the Palmerston murder and it's only a matter o' time afore they find out about Sloane Beaumont.'

'Aye, someone once said that when more than five people ken a secret, it'll no' be a secret much longer.'

'Up here,' Hamish said, 'when more than one person kens a secret it'll no' be a secret once the pub opens. What worries me is that, when the roads are clear and you can get here, so can the press. They'll descend on us like a plague. They're already having a field day wi' this one and it's no' yet been twenty-four hours since Palmerston was murdered.'

'Aye, we made twenty-eight arrests in a major crime operation and all the hacks are interested in is the "Wedding Day Murder". I'll take care o' the press, laddie. You concentrate on pulling together as much information and evidence as you can. Any idea who the murderer might be?' Jimmy asked.

'We've a shortlist o' suspects. I'm trying to narrow it down a wee bit afore you get here.'

'Do you think we're looking at a lone killer, or more than one?'

'Hard to say at the moment, Jimmy, but I'll ken more when I've spoken to a few more o' the folk we're most interested in.'

'Keep at it, Hamish,' Jimmy said.

When they finished their call, Hamish opened his laptop and trawled the Police National Computer database, firing a few names at it to see what turned up. One of the results was interesting and he finished making notes just as Davey showed up with the Ferguson brothers.

'Why don't you have a talk wi' John in the bar, Constable Forbes?' Hamish suggested. 'Leave Alan in here wi' me.'

Alan Ferguson sat at the table, still dressed in the black suit, black tie and black hat he'd been wearing in the Blues Mobile the previous day, although now he had added black sunglasses.

'Finding it a bit bright in here, are you, Alan?' Hamish asked, indicating the sunglasses.

'They're part o' the outfit we wear,' Alan grunted.

'Take them off,' Hamish ordered.

Alan reluctantly removed the sunglasses to reveal that his left cheek was looking slightly pink and swollen.

'Is that from where Darius Palmerston thumped you in reception?' Hamish asked.

'It was a cheap shot – caught me by surprise. I'd have given him a right pasting if John hadn't stepped in.'

'I'm sure you would,' Hamish said, glancing down at his notes. 'Your record would back that up. It's littered wi' arrests for affray and assault, wi' a number o' convictions and even a couple o' spells in the jail. Apparently you worked as a bouncer at one o' the Macgregors' clubs.'

'Aye, that was me a few years back,' Alan admitted. 'It's no' me any more, but I've no' forgotten how to fight. Yon was the Englishman's lucky day.'

'No' so lucky really, though, was it?' Hamish said. 'A few minutes later he was lying carved up on the breakfast-room floor.'

'That had nothing to do wi' me!' Alan growled.

'Aye, right,' Hamish said. 'So you say. What were you arguing wi' Palmerston about?'

'We had all our gear in the van outside, ready to set up,' Alan said. 'We wanted to take a quick look at the room to see how best to bring all our stuff in but the woman who organises everything here wasn't around. We thought we'd go into the bar for a quick drink but then *he* came walking past and told us he didn't want "scum" like us in the same bar as his wedding guests.'

'And you took exception to that?' Hamish asked.

'Too right, I did!' Alan replied. 'I wasn't taking shite like that from a stuck-up English prick like him! I told him what I thought o' him, there was a wee bit o' pushing and shoving and I took a smack in the face.'

'What happened then?'

'He disappeared and the woman turned up. She showed John and me the back corridor – it goes to the kitchens – where we could see what we needed to. We took a look while the rest o' the band went off down the pub. We had a smoke somewhere out the back o' the hotel while I put some snow on my face to calm it down. Then we walked back through to the reception area and joined the lads in the pub.'

'And, of course, your brother will vouch for all that.'

'Of course.'

'All right, Alan, as soon as Davey's finished wi' John, you can go.'

'How about a lift back?' Alan asked.

'We're no' a taxi service.'

'These weren't made for walking on snow,' Alan said, pulling his leg up clear of the table to point at his black, thin-soled leather shoes. 'You folk brought me here. If I slip and break my leg because you've forced me to walk back, I'll sue.'

Hamish sighed and got to his feet, taking Alan Ferguson out into the reception area where he told him to wait with his brother while he conferred with Davey in the incident room.

'What did you get from him?' Hamish asked Davey.

'John says Alan was a bad lad in the past, but since he formed the band and took him under his wing, he's left all that behind him,' Davey replied, going on to run through the story John Ferguson had given him about the events of the previous day.

'Same story as Alan's,' Hamish said. 'Practically word-for-word. Well-rehearsed.'

'Or true,' Davey suggested.

'Aye, maybe,' Hamish said. 'Take them back to Mrs Mackenzie's place, Davey, and then find me Donald Maclean.'

Hamish walked out to reception with Davey, who took the two black-suited Ferguson brothers out to the Land Rover. Scouting the office and then the bar, Hamish found Silas in a quiet corner, checking through a phone. He looked up as Hamish approached.

'I can't see anything of interest to us on this one,' he said, dropping it back into its plastic bag and removing his gloves. 'You know, Hamish, by rights I shouldn't be looking at any of the phones at all.'

'Aye, I ken that fine,' Hamish said, 'but needs must and we'll keep it to ourselves in any case. I want to talk to Serena Hamilton next. You've seen far more o' her than I have. How is she reacting to the murder?'

'She's a strange one. I know I said she looked like she'd been having it away wi' Darius,' Silas said, 'but she's no' seemed that upset about him being killed. She's acting just the same as always.'

'And how is that, exactly?' Hamish asked.

'She's cold as yon snow outside,' Silas said. 'Nothing fazes her and she treats the staff here like servants.'

'Well, she's married to the top man,' Hamish said. 'I suppose she's used to being treated like the queen o' the castle.'

'Aye and that's all very well,' Silas said, 'but she shouldn't look down her nose at the rest of us. There's another thing – the nose. The more I look at her the more I can see that it's no' just the make-up propping up her looks. Her face doesn't move right. I think there's a lot of work been done and a lot of money been spent to keep her looking good.'

'Each to their own,' Hamish said with a shrug. 'If it makes her happy, where's the harm?'

'Och, I think folk should let themselves grow older at their own pace,' Silas said, 'not pick up the phone to a surgeon every time a wee wrinkle appears.'

'Well, I'd like to see her wrinkle-free face in the incident room as soon as you like, please, Silas,' Hamish said. 'Alan Ferguson just told me he and his brother went out the back o' the hotel for a smoke,' he added as an afterthought. 'Would that be on camera?'

'Not necessarily,' Silas said. 'It's something I've been trying to get Priscilla to improve. We don't have full coverage round the back. In fact, there's more blind spots than there is coverage.'

'Okay, Silas,' Hamish said. 'Let's see the glamorous Mrs Hamilton.'

'Right you are, Hamish,' Silas said. 'Once I've brought her down, I'll nip up to the roof for a wee look. I need to make sure the snow's no' too heavy for the flat parts and no' about to slide down the sloping parts and rip off the guttering.'

On his way back to the incident room, Hamish met Priscilla and Helen standing at the reception desk. Helen was holding a small, white envelope.

'Sergeant, I know you want us all to stay in our rooms . . .' she began, '. . . but obviously, my room is . . . anyway, I thought I should give you this. She offered him the envelope. 'Sloane gave it to me just before we left for the church with Alannah. She said it was personal and I was touched because I thought it was a gift for me . . . and I hadn't thought to get her anything, so it was a little embarrassing. I got round to opening it this morning and, actually, I don't think it was meant as a gift for me at all. I think these are Sloane's keepsakes, maybe good-luck tokens, and she simply didn't have room for the envelope in her handbag. I think, perhaps, these should go with the rest of Sloane's things when . . . you know . . . it's all gathered together.'

'Thank you, miss,' Hamish said, taking the envelope and slotting it into a pocket. 'I'll take good care o' it.'

Hamish had scarcely sat down at the incident room table before Serena Hamilton waltzed in, looking back over her shoulder.

'I'd like coffee,' she commanded Silas. 'Don't bother with that rubbish at the bar. I don't want that muck. Get me coffee from the kitchen where the chef keeps the decent stuff.'

'You know Silas is the hotel security manager, no' a waiter?' Hamish said, watching Serena arrange herself in the seat opposite his. 'He's got a lot to do right now.'

'Sergeant, I think you're confusing me with someone who gives a shit,' Serena said, coolly. 'You don't expect me to fetch my own coffee, do you?'

'Perish the thought . . .' Hamish said, flicking open his

notebook. 'Now, Mrs Hamilton, I just want to go over a few things from your initial statement for the crime team who'll be arriving later.'

'I'll tell you what I can,' Serena said, lifting her handbag from her lap onto the table and producing a red-and-gold pack of Dunhill cigarettes.

'You can't smoke in here, Mrs Hamilton, or in any other indoor public spaces in the hotel,' Hamish warned her. 'That's the law.'

'I'm not stupid, Sergeant!' she snapped. 'I like to take my coffee with a pack of cigarettes sitting beside it to remind me of the time when we all had the freedom to do what the hell we liked in this country.'

'As you will,' Hamish said, shrugging. 'So, where were you when Darius Palmerston was murdered?'

'I'd gone up to my room to change my dress and my shoes,' she replied. 'The dress wasn't suitable for the ceilidh and the heels I'd had on at the church and during the meal were causing me agony. I wanted to wear something more practical. While I was up there, I had a cigarette on the balcony.'

'When did you first meet Darius?'

'I think it was when Alannah had some of her friends down for a weekend house party at our estate in Hampshire a couple of years ago,' Serena said, tapping her manicured fingernails on her cigarette pack to help summon the memory. 'Yes, definitely then. We keep a flat in Mayfair as well, but it's a little cramped for entertaining. Much nicer to have space for everyone to spread out and relax.'

'What was your impression of him?'

'I don't do impressions.'

Hamish stared at her, blankly.

'That was my little joke, Sergeant,' she explained.

'Och, right, of course,' Hamish said, forcing a laugh. 'What I meant was, what did you think o' him?'

'He was utterly charming – so much more mature than the rest of her little gang.'

'What made you think that?'

'He knew how to talk to a lady, Sergeant. He knew how to treat a lady. He was considerate and polite and, when he chose to be, quite sharp with his witty remarks. He was clearly very intelligent and struck me as a man who knew what he wanted and knew where he was going in life.'

'That's a lot to take in from one brief meeting,' Hamish observed.

'Well, we started to see a good deal more of him once he and Alannah were dating.'

'I see. Can you recall who else was at that first house party?'

'Some of those who are up here, Sergeant. Sebastian, of course – Darius never went anywhere without him – and Richard Wade, who never goes anywhere without Simon. Funny how some blokes like to go around in pairs, isn't it? It was quite a coup to have Richard there – not everyone can say they had a viscount at the weekend.'

'There must have been some ladies there, too,' Hamish said.

'Naturally, Sergeant. I'm sure Helen was there . . . and Sloane.' Serena paused as if waiting for a reaction from Hamish. She didn't get one.

'Not Priscilla?' Hamish asked.

'Not Priscilla,' she replied with a snide smile. 'She wasn't really part of the gang. Truth be told, she's still a bit of an outsider.'

Silas arrived carrying a small tray loaded with a pot of coffee, two bone-china cups standing proudly in saucers, a bowl of sugar and a small jug of cream. He looked at the cigarettes on the table and then towards Hamish, who gave a slight shake of his head. Silas placed the tray on the table and left without saying a word, heading off to check the snow on the roof.

'Allow me, Mrs Hamilton,' Hamish said, standing to set her cup in front of her and pour her coffee. He poured a cup for himself and offered her sugar and cream. She took neither. He took both.

'You say Darius and Sebastian were inseparable. I take it you got to know Sebastian quite well, too?'

'Nobody gets to know Sebastian very well,' she answered, laughing. 'He's a bit of a closed book. Darius was the only one who could read him and he adored Darius. If you got him on his own, Seb either struggled to make conversation or would repeat things he'd heard Darius say. He even adopted the same sort of tone as Darius. If you really wanted someone to do an impression of Darius, Seb would be your man, although you'd never get him to do it. When he was talking like Darius, the poor boy obviously didn't even realise he was doing it.'

'Those two were very close, then,' Hamish commented.

'Like brothers,' Serena confirmed, 'but not really like brothers. Anybody who'd seen them together will tell you the same – Darius treated Seb like his personal servant. Seb did everything Darius told him to do. Pour me more coffee.'

'The pot's right by you, Mrs Hamilton,' Hamish pointed out. 'Please feel free to help yourself.'

Serena laughed and pointed a finger at Hamish to emphasise what she said next.

'You see?' she said. 'You can deflect an offhand command like that, no problem at all. If Darius had said that to Seb – and he said things like that to him all the time – Seb would have got up and poured him some coffee. It was a bit of a joke in Alannah's friendship group that Seb was Darius's little slave.'

'His slave?' Hamish raised his eyebrows. 'That doesn't sound like they were such good friends after all.'

'Oh, but they were, Sergeant,' she assured him. 'Seb would have been totally lost without Darius and I don't . . .' Her voice cracked, as though she had just realised what she was about to say and the words had stuck in her throat. She took a sip of coffee. 'I don't know what he's going to do now. I can't think what will become of him without Darius.'

'Do you think they were more than just friends?' Hamish asked.

'If you're implying that they were gay, Sergeant, then you're way off the mark,' Serena said. 'They had a special bond – actually more like the brothers scenario. Seb was the weaker of the two. He relied on Darius and Darius looked after him. Being there for Seb seemed to give Darius a purpose in life.'

'How did you feel when Alannah became engaged to Darius?' he asked.

'I was very pleased for them – especially pleased for Alannah, of course,' she replied. 'You see, Sergeant, Alannah and I are very close. She may be a little younger . . .' she looked across at Hamish as though expecting a compliment about her not looking any older, got no response and moved on, 'but, rather than stepmother and stepdaughter, we're really more like sisters.

'We regularly go into town together to go shopping

and take in a show. I so love the theatre, don't you? I worked in the arts for a while and the theatre is my passion. Alannah and I see all the top shows in the West End – that's in London, you know. It's the main reason we kept our flat in Mayfair.

'Charles isn't so enamoured of the arts and would rather spend time at his club when he's in London, talking business and smoking cigars, which he shouldn't really do with his heart condition. He uses that as an excuse not to travel as well. I often end up taking short holidays all on my own.

'Darius wasn't a bit like Charles. He's a member of some London club or other, but he'd always be there when we met up with Alannah's friends for drinks before a show. It was a joy to see how her face lit up when Darius spoke to her. So, as you can probably tell, I was thrilled for them when they became engaged. He was a wonderful man.'

'Your husband doesn't actually share your opinion o' Darius,' Hamish told her, looking at his notes. 'He described Darius as "a complete scoundrel".'

Serena laughed out loud.

'Oh, that's such a "Charles" word,' she said, calming herself by fanning a hand in front of her face. '"Scoundrel!" Who else would say such a thing?'

'He said that Darius had run up debts all over Europe,' Hamish informed her. 'Leaving hotel rooms without paying – all sorts o' shenanigans.'

'I know all about that,' she said, waving her hand as if to dismiss the matter. 'Darius told me about it. He had a bit of a wild time down on the Med for a while, but that's all being taken care of. I mean to say, you have to live a little when you're young, don't you? Lean slightly off the rails, get into a little hot water – it's how we learn about responsibility.'

'You clearly liked Darius a lot,' Hamish said.

'I did,' she said, suddenly looking glum.

'Given that you and Alannah are like . . . sisters, did you ever think o' Darius in a . . . romantic way?'

She picked up her cigarette packet and began turning it end over end, tapping it on the table.

'I'm a married woman, Sergeant,' she said, her voice flat and cold. 'If you're asking me if I had an affair with Darius Palmerston, then the answer is no. It's one thing to live a little, but another to be reckless. Living a little can get you a slap on the wrist – being reckless can lose you everything.'

Hamish stared across the table at her, his head cocked slightly to one side. Not for the first time during their conversation, he could plainly see she wasn't telling the truth. The defiant look in her eyes said she was lying and challenged him to prove it.

'If that's all, Sergeant, then I will now go and have a cigarette in my room where there is a small balcony,' she said. 'I can enjoy the cigarette, the view and the room, all paid for in advance – no shenanigans.'

She put her cigarettes back in her bag, got up and walked to the door where she stopped and looked back at Hamish. He returned her gaze for a heartbeat, then laughed and rushed over to grab the door handle.

'*Do* allow me, Mrs Hamilton,' he said, bowing theatrically and opening the door.

She tutted, rolled her eyes and stalked out. Hamish leant against the doorpost, thinking, then walked out of the hotel and round to the raised terrace where Hamilton and Jensen had stood smoking their cigars the previous day. From there he could see out over the loch to the mountains beyond, their snow shrouds having lost their sparkle beneath the grey clouds that hugged their peaks.

In his head, he ran through the conversation he had just had with Serena Hamilton. He tried to tick off all the places where he thought she'd been lying, or at least embellishing the truth. He settled on her two main lies having been about when she first met Darius and the whopper about the affair.

'Ah, you're round here,' said Davey, following Hamish's tracks through the snow. 'Donald is out wi' Archie on the boat, but they're due back soon. I managed to get him on the phone and he said he'd come straight here as soon as they dock.'

'That gives us a bit o' time to think,' Hamish said, 'and sort out where we've got to so far. Let's get back inside. A breath o' fresh air clears your heid but when it's this cold it's liable to freeze your lungs at the same time.'

Silas, fresh from the roof, was crossing reception when Hamish and Davey walked back in. Hamish asked him to join them in the incident room.

'All o' Jimmy's boys are keeping themselves occupied,' Silas reported. 'We still have one down at the bridge, one's wi' Chalmers in Freddy's room and the other two are prowling the corridors. They know they'll be relieved when Jimmy arrives wi' more men, so they've abandoned the shifts.'

'Fair enough,' Hamish said. 'Now – here's what we have from those I've spoken to so far. Let's start wi' the bridesmaid, Helen Carter. She's a bonny lass and to me she seems honest as the day is long, but we don't know where she was at the time o' the murder and she's definitely hiding something.'

'I can't imagine her doing that to Darius,' Davey said.

'And she was properly fond o' Sloane,' Silas said. 'She doesn't strike me as a cold-blooded killer.'

'These may no' have been cold-blooded murders,' Hamish pointed out. 'From what we're hearing about the love lives o' these folk, passions may have been running high. We can't discount her until we know what her secret is.'

'Then there's Priscilla,' Davey said, 'but she's not a murderer.'

'Priscilla had a fling wi' Darius,' Hamish said. The other two looked at each other in disbelief. 'I told you passions were running high around here,' Hamish went on. 'The relationship ended some time ago but, if we're being objective, we can't discount jealousy and betrayal as motives and she has no real alibi. Priscilla remains a suspect.'

'Paul Hunter fits the bill,' Silas offered. 'No credible alibi, hated Darius, is in love wi' Alannah, had bloodstained clothes and tried to make a run for it.'

'Agreed,' Hamish said. 'It doesn't look good for Paul, but why would he kill Sloane? He seemed genuinely surprised and upset when he found out she was dead. He immediately blamed it on "them".'

'Could they have been Hamilton and Jensen?' asked Davey. 'What motive would they have had?'

'Hamilton might have found out about Darius and Serena,' Silas offered. 'He could have flown into a rage and murdered him – a true crime of passion. If Sloane saw what happened, they might have wanted to eliminate the witness and could have done for her, too.'

'I suppose it's possible,' Hamish said. 'Hamilton was cagey when I talked to him and Jensen is a cocky devil, but he had an explanation for the "terminate him" chat. Given how sensitive Hamilton is to bad publicity, I can't imagine he would ever have done something like this on his daughter's wedding day. I think they're now low-level suspects.'

'What about Serena herself?' Davey asked.

'She's definitely up to something,' Hamish replied. 'She lied to me more than once and from the look she gave me when she denied having an affair wi' Darius, I'd say it was a safe bet there was something going on between them. Then there's this.'

Hamish opened his iPad to display the photographs he'd taken of the torn Valentine's card.

'The envelope's addressed "D" and the card's signed "S",' Davey said. 'Given that you found it in his room, it's obvious it was given to Darius, but who is "S"?'

'It could be Serena,' Silas reasoned, 'or it might even be Sloane.'

'Sloane Beaumont liked a bit o' fun,' Hamish said, 'but I doubt it was from her – no' unless it was a joke. She must have been killed for a reason, but she wouldn't have been carrying on wi' her best friend's fiancé.'

'Would Serena be daft enough to send Darius a Valentine's card on his wedding day?' Silas wondered.

'Maybe,' Hamish said. 'She's arrogant enough to do that and see it as one o' her own "little jokes".'

'Of course,' Silas said, thoughtfully, 'the card might have been from Sebastian.'

'Blokes don't send each other Valentine's cards,' Davey said, scoffing.

'Get your head in the twenty-first century, Davey,' Silas said. 'Men can be wi' men and even get married nowadays. You have to be thinking in the modern era.

This is a double murder investigation and we need to keep an open mind about everything.'

'Silas begins with an "S",' Davey said and both he and Hamish turned to Silas with grave expressions.

'What . . . ?' Silas said. 'Surely you don't think that . . .'

Hamish and Davey burst out laughing and Silas let out a sigh, shaking his head.

'This is one o' the reasons I never got on as a policeman,' he said. 'You folk can be having a laugh when even the most awful things are happening all around you.'

'It's how we keep ourselves sane, Silas,' Davey said, slapping him on the shoulder.

'From everything that Serena said,' Hamish said, still chuckling, 'and from what we know about her relationship wi' Darius, we can be pretty sure that he wasn't gay. She's so catty that, had she even suspected Sebastian was gay, I think she would have alluded to it. None o' the others have mentioned anything like that either in their initial statements or in the interviews we've done. I think we can rule out Darius and Sebastian being gay. Their relationship was more complicated than that.'

'Which means we still don't know who the card was from,' Silas said, looking at the photograph. 'The handwriting could be anyone's.'

'We also have that text message from Sebastian to Darius,' Davey said. '"SHE KNOWS," but we've still no idea what it means.'

'That's something for me to press Sebastian on when I have another talk wi' him,' Hamish said. 'Then there's Alan Ferguson. Darius walloped him, so he might have been out for revenge, but that might all have been some kind o' set up. He's a man wi' a short temper and a criminal record and he was involved wi' some o' the most violent gangs down in Glasgow.'

'Not the Macgregors again,' Davey said.

'Aye,' Hamish replied. 'They're a nasty bunch and they've a way o' reaching out when they have business to deal wi'.'

'Business?' Silas sounded confused. 'Are you talking about Darius's debts? Do you think he might have been killed because he owed money to the wrong people?'

'That seems a bit far-fetched,' Davey said.

'It does,' Hamish agreed, 'but I wouldn't put anything past the Macgregors. Ferguson remains a suspect.'

Mr Johnson knocked and stuck his head round the door.

'There's a Mr Maclean here to see you, Hamish,' he said.

'Thank you, Mr Johnson,' Hamish said. 'Send him in. Lads, I'll deal wi' Donald on my own.'

Davey left with Silas and Donald Maclean walked in wearing a heavy yellow oilskin jacket, open to reveal a sweater that looked so thick it might have been knitted from rope. Clearly he'd rushed straight to the hotel as soon as *Bluebell* had docked.

'Take off yon coat, Donald, and the jumper. You'll be fainting wi' the heat in here wi' those on,' Hamish said.

Donald did as he was told, then sat in the chair indicated by Hamish.

'Donald, you're here because you've managed to make yourself a suspect in a murder enquiry,' Hamish told him. 'Have you any idea what a serious thing that is?'

'Aye,' Donald said, quietly, staring at the table.

'You were seen having an altercation wi' the deceased – Darius Palmerston – in the Piper on Thursday night,'

Hamish informed him. 'What's worse, you were seen by *me*! Witnesses state that you then had a further shouting match wi' him on your uncle Archie's boat the very next day. Furthermore, you stated that evening that if he annoyed you just one more time you would kill him.'

'Who told you that?' Donald said, looking up in alarm.

'It doesn't matter who told me,' Hamish said. 'Anybody could have told me. You've lived in Lochdubh all your days. You grew up here. You should know that, day or night, rain or shine, there will *always* be someone in the village who sees what you do or hears what you say – and you said you would kill Darius Palmerston!'

'Aye, I killed him,' Donald said with anger in his eyes. 'I battered him wi' a bar stool, I drowned him in the loch, I strangled him wi' my bare hands. I killed him a hundred times in my heid, but in the real world I never laid a hand on the man!'

'Don't play games, laddie,' Hamish warned him. 'You could be in enough trouble as it is. Did you say that you would kill Palmerston?'

'It's true,' Donald said, hanging his head in shame. 'I did say I would kill him, but I didn't mean I would actually *kill* him. It's just a figure o' speech.'

'Figure o' speech?' Hamish sounded flabbergasted. 'How does "life sentence" sound as a figure o' speech? Tell me where you were when Palmerston was killed.'

'Well, I had a wee dram or two when I got home,' Donald explained, 'and fell asleep in front o' the telly. When I woke up it was near time to get up anyway and I was fair starving so I made myself a massive fry-up for breakfast. Well, when I started working at the hotel, there were all these wee snacks to serve folk, and they were right tasty, so I had a few o' them. Then we were given our lunch and that was no' something to turn down either so I was totally stuffed and I had to pay a visit to—'

'Donald, are you telling me you were sitting on the toilet when Palmerston was murdered?'

'Aye,' Donald nodded sheepishly, 'and there were no witnesses.'

'I should hope not!' Hamish barked. 'Take your coat and yon jumper and get out o' my sight afore I can think o' something to charge you wi'!'

Donald was scooping his sweater up off the floor when Jimmy's young PC, Rory, burst in.

'Sergeant Macbeth!' he gasped, as though he'd run a marathon. 'I've found the missing kilt – and it's a right gory sight!'

Chapter Nine

If there were no bad people, there would be no good lawyers.
Charles Dickens, *The Old Curiosity Shop* (1841)

Rory led Hamish out into the snow and round to the stable block. Beyond the stables and the bedsit used by Paul Hunter was a cluster of sheds, outbuildings for storing equipment used by the gardeners. The wooden buildings normally stood slightly clear of the ground, the floor joists supported on concrete blocks to create a gap that allowed air to circulate beneath, keeping the floors dry and sound. Wire mesh was used in an effort to stop the local wildlife making their homes under the sheds. Now, however, the snow had more than closed the gap, piling up against the mesh, and the sheds were beginning to look slightly buried.

Hamish and Rory stopped about five metres from the sheds while Hamish surveyed the scene. Most of the mesh and the gap below the sheds were hidden by the depth of the snow but there was one obvious part, to which Rory was now needlessly pointing, where the snow had been dug away and the mesh ripped asunder. The snow near the damage had been trampled and the tartan of the kilt Sebastian had been wearing at the wedding was in plain sight. The area on which the kilt was lying was coloured with pink smears and stains where blood from the kilt had leached into the snow.

'I came out for a bit o' fresh air,' Rory explained, 'and to check around the building, when I saw that. I went up to identify what it was, but I didn't touch anything.'

'Right,' Hamish said, stepping forward to follow Rory's footsteps towards the kilt. 'You bide here, Rory. I'll take a wee look.'

Hamish walked to the edge of the patch of disturbed snow. Rory's fresh footprints were obvious but any older ones had been covered by the snow that had fallen overnight. The only other discernible marks were animal tracks. He took out his phone and crouched down to examine the kilt. He photographed an area where the kilt's woollen weave was torn and mangled. To the side of the kilt lay the sealskin sporran. There were bite marks and bits that had been chewed away. Stooping so low that his ear almost touched the snow, Hamish could see past the excavated snow beneath the shed where the rest of Sebastian's outfit appeared to have been hidden along with a shredded carrier bag. He stood up and retraced his steps to where Rory was waiting.

'I want you to stand guard here, Rory,' he said. 'Don't let anyone near the kilt or yon sheds. We'll let the crime team deal wi' it all when they get here from Strathbane. I'll have one o' your pals come out to take ower in a couple o' hours. Well spotted, lad.'

He left Rory standing guard and made his way back to the incident room where Davey and Silas were waiting with Elspeth.

'Hamish, Jensen says he'll sack me if I don't put together a video report for him,' Elspeth said. 'Frankly, he's been such a pain over all this, I'm about ready to hand my notice in anyway.'

'Don't do that, Elspeth,' Hamish said, taking a deep breath. 'The story's out now, so you might as well do something wi' some o' the recordings you've got. I trust you not to include anything that might compromise the investigation, and we don't want to give away anything about Sloane until Jimmy authorises it. I'll make sure he gives you the first interview as soon as he gets here.'

Elspeth thanked him and went off to start compiling her report. Hamish sat down at the table and showed the other two the photographs on his phone.

'It looks to me like Chalmers's outfit, most definitely stained wi' blood, was hidden under the sheds outside,' he said. 'Somebody ripped the wire mesh away and stuffed everything in there, then forced the mesh back in place. The falling snow then covered their tracks.

'Unfortunately for whoever hid the things there, a fox later came along, attracted by the scent o' blood. Clearly it thought it had an easy meal tucked away under the shed. It managed to haul the mesh aside again and drag the kilt and sporran out. It had a wee go at it but I'm guessing it abandoned the outfit because it knew there were easier and tastier pickings to be had at the hotel bins.'

'So we have Sebastian's outfit stained wi' blood,' Silas said, 'and Paul's outfit also bloodstained.'

'But we're not able to tell yet whose blood it is,' Davey said. 'Without forensics we don't know which clothes have Darius's blood and which clothes have Sloane's.'

'They could each have a mixture of both,' Silas offered.

'That would suggest Sebastian and Paul were working together,' Hamish said.

'Which does fit with some scenarios,' Davey agreed. 'Hiding Sloane's body in that broom cupboard would have been far easier for two people.'

'Aye, but why would they be wanting to kill Darius and Sloane?' Hamish pondered.

'If Sloane saw them kill Darius,' Silas said, 'they couldn't let her escape as a witness. They might have chased her upstairs and killed her to keep her quiet.'

'That's the thing, though,' Hamish argued, 'she wouldn't have been quiet. If Sloane had witnessed Darius being hacked at wi' yon sword, she'd have screamed the place down and everyone would have come running through from the dining room.'

'It doesn't make sense for them both to have got bloodied if they weren't working together,' said Silas. 'I can't believe they both independently chose to go out and commit murder right here yesterday.'

'They also hid their bloodstained clothes in much the same area,' Davey said. 'That surely can't be a coincidence. It makes it look like they were in the same place at the same time, given that there must be thousands of potential hiding places in the hotel and the grounds.'

'True,' Hamish agreed, 'but one set o' clothes was far better hidden than the other, was it no'? Why would that be?'

'Who knows what they were thinking?' Silas said. 'Maybe they were panicking. They had to hide their clothes quickly and they probably expected that the police would go over the whole hotel from top to bottom searching for clues.'

'We might have done,' Davey said. 'Under normal circumstances, that might well have been what *would* have happened. If the whole hotel was a crime scene, everyone might have been evacuated into custody in Strathbane while it was searched. Maybe the killers planned to escape on the way, but an evacuation didn't happen because we were snowed in and there wasn't the manpower.'

'I think you're straying off track now, lads,' Hamish said. 'You're thinking like all this was planned and it can't have been. It's too chaotic. You don't plan to kill someone wi' a sword when there's a room full o' people right next door.'

'None o' it makes sense really, does it?' Silas said.

'No' yet,' Hamish said, 'but it will. We just need to find something that pulls it all together, so we'll carry on talking to folk. Silas, can you fetch Darius's cousins, Stephen Palmerston and Henry Poulter, down here, please?'

The two young men were slim, fresh-faced and dark-haired. Looking at them, Hamish reckoned that, had he not known they were related, he could probably have guessed. They were both nineteen years old, had the same look across the eyes and bridge of the nose, the same heavy eyebrows and the same easy smile.

'Thanks for coming down, lads,' he said, having opted for him and Davey to interview them both together. 'This must all have been a real shock for you.'

'It's certainly been a weekend I'll never forget,' Stephen said.

'Me neither,' Henry agreed. 'We came up here because we thought it would be a bit of a laugh and the whole thing's turned massive! Totally lit!'

'Aye, right,' Hamish said, frowning. 'Is that a good or a bad thing?'

The two youngsters laughed.

'When we get back to uni in Bath,' Stephen said, 'our flatmates are going to be green with envy that we got to be in the middle of all this while they were just hanging in the same old bars.'

'So you're at university together?' Davey asked.

'Yeah, pretty much by accident,' Henry replied. 'We didn't really even know each other before uni, then our mothers found out we were both going to Bath and put us in touch. We were cool with that.'

'I knew I had a couple of cousins somewhere,' Henry said, 'but I never thought I'd end up at uni with one.'

'And Darius Palmerston was also a cousin to both of you?' asked Hamish.

'That's how we came to get invited here,' Stephen said. 'Actually, we weren't invited. My mum was, but my gran said that if she went to the wedding of Darius Palmerston, she'd never speak to her again.'

'Same here!' Henry laughed. 'All our family saw him as a real dodgy character. They hated him but we'd never even met him. We were nominated to come up here and represent the family.'

'How did you feel about that?' Davey asked.

'Brilliant!' Stephen answered. 'We were bought new suits and sent up here, all expenses paid and it's been champagne and whisky all the way. What could possibly go wrong?'

'How about a murder?' Hamish suggested.

'Ah, yes, that put a real downer on everything,' Henry said, as if suddenly remembering the events of the past twenty-four hours. 'Horrible. My mum was expecting a full report on the beautiful wedding when we got back. When I tell her what actually happened, she's going to freak.'

'What did your family have against Darius?' Hamish asked.

'According to what we've been told,' Stephen said, 'his parents died when he was about our age. They lived in a big house and had made a bomb when they sold their computer company. They told everyone that, when they passed, they'd make sure everybody in the family got some benefit from their success.'

'When they actually died, though,' Henry took up the story, 'there was a funeral and then Darius and his creepy mate Seb took off with all the money and joined the army.'

'The house was sold and everything,' Stephen said. 'Nobody ever heard from Darius again until now. My mum said old man Hamilton insisted that there should be someone from our side at the wedding, just for appearances' sake.'

'Why do you think Sebastian is creepy?' asked Davey.

'It's just the way he's been this weekend. He never said much when Darius was around,' Stephen said, 'and he stuck to Darius like glue. He did everything Darius said, like he was some kind of android.'

'And when Darius wasn't around,' Henry added, 'he acted just like him. We called him "Darius Light" – just like the real thing but with none of the flavour!'

They both laughed and Hamish waved a finger at them.

'This is a serious matter, lads – a murder enquiry,' he said, 'so less o' the clowning around. Where were you when Darius was murdered?'

'We went out through the breakfast room and across the terrace into part of the garden. I guess it's a lawn but it's covered in snow,' Stephen said.

'And what did you do there?' Davey asked.

'We ran around in the snow and threw snowballs,' Henry said, folding his arms. 'We don't really get snow where we live. I've only ever seen snow three times in my whole life and it wasn't nearly as deep as it is here.'

Hamish stared at him and Henry's eyes flicked to Stephen, then he shifted uncomfortably, unfolded his arms and stuffed his hands in his pockets.

'Aye, right,' Hamish said, shaking his head and moving his gaze to Stephen. 'Now tell me what you were really doing.'

'We really did throw a few snowballs,' Stephen said, with a heavy sigh, 'and we shared a spliff.'

'That's better,' Hamish said. 'We'll get along just fine as long as you tell me the truth. What happened next?'

'When we tried to get back in through the breakfast room, the doors were locked,' Henry said.

'We went along the kitchen corridor and into the dining room that way,' Stephen said. 'That's when we found out what had happened.'

'Did you see anybody else when you were coming back in?' Davey asked.

'Only Serena Hamilton,' Henry answered. 'She went into the dining room from the kitchen corridor just ahead of us.'

'That'll do, for now,' Hamish said. 'Silas will take you two back to your room but listen, lads – double wrap your stash. The major crime team is arriving from Strathbane later and they can smell the wacky baccy a mile off.'

Stephen and Henry looked at each other with huge relief, got to their feet as quickly as they could and headed for the door.

'Will we have their wee garden jaunt on camera?' Hamish asked Davey as the two young men left.

'The snow was falling so hard that the cameras were only really picking up what was right in front of them,'

Davey said, 'but we might find something. What was all that about the major crime team?'

'Those two are young and enjoying their lives,' Hamish said. 'So they've got a bit o' weed wi' them – what do I care? Maybe I just gave them a bit o' an idea that ordinary police officers understand them and can be trusted. There's no harm in that. What did you think about what they had to say?'

'I think their story sounded plausible – and they kind of confirmed Serena's story, too.'

'They confirmed she probably used the backstairs to reach her room and came back that way,' Hamish said.

'That's the quickest way from the dining room to her room,' Davey said.

'Aye, but knowing she went that way and knowing what she did when she was upstairs are two different things,' Hamish said. He stood up and paced around the room. 'There's an awfy lot we need to find out afore we can sort out this mess.'

'How much more do we need to sort out?' Davey said. 'We might already have the two murderers in custody. Paul's locked in the cell down at the station and Chalmers is under guard in Freddy's room.'

'Aye, and we appear to have evidence against both o' them,' Hamish said, 'but the trail doesn't end wi' those two and they don't sit well together as partners in crime. I don't think they worked together to kill Palmerston and Sloane. The big question remains, who did do it?'

There came a knock at the door and Priscilla walked in.

'I need to know what we should do about lunch,' she said. 'Whatever we decide, Freddy needs time to prepare. We have to provide for our guests.'

'Lunch?' Hamish was flabbergasted. 'No, I'm no' having them all wandering about the hotel yet again. Can they no' make do wi' sandwiches in their rooms?'

'Do you intend to hold everyone prisoner?' Priscilla demanded.

'Do you intend to let a potential murderer loose among your other guests?' Hamish countered. 'Yes, I *do* want to keep them all locked up safe and sound! I should probably have locked the place down at breakfast as well, but now they can all bide where they are until we have more police here for security!'

'Very well,' Priscilla said, with a haughty sniff, 'I'll tell our enormously talented, hugely creative head chef to . . . butter some bread.'

Realising he'd been too harsh with her, Hamish got up to try to pacify Priscilla, following her out of the room but catching no more than an icy blast of cold shoulder. He then saw an eager Silas, leaning against the reception desk, awaiting instructions.

'Silas, it's starting to feel like I'm having you feed these folk in on a conveyor belt,' he said, 'but I think I want to speak to Viscount Carsely next.'

'Should I invite the Honourable Simon Derringer as well?' Silas asked.

'The what?' Hamish frowned. 'What the hell's an Honourable?'

'It's a thing they tack on to the names o' the children o' viscounts and barons or the younger sons o' earls,' Silas said, congratulating himself on having looked it up.

'Just Richard Wade, please, Silas,' Hamish said.

A few minutes later, Viscount Carsely walked into the incident room along with the Honourable Simon Derringer.

'I hope you don't mind Simon joining us for this interview, Sergeant,' Wade said. 'He's not just my friend, you see, he's also my lawyer.'

'You've not been cautioned and nor are you under arrest,' Hamish replied. 'This is no' that kind o' an interview. You're simply helping us wi' our enquiries. Also, in Scotland, I decide when you get to have a lawyer present.'

'I'm a little rusty on Scots law and procedure, Sergeant,' Simon said, smiling politely, 'but as this is just an extended statement, I don't think there's any real problem about me sitting in.'

'We're not trying to be awkward,' Wade said, taking a seat as if to show that he was keen to stay. 'I want to help and I'm always happier if Simon sits in on meetings.'

'Why's that?' Hamish asked.

'Because there are people who like to take advantage,' Wade said. 'To you, I might look like an overprivileged toff, but I have to think about more than just myself. I feel very much responsible for the livelihoods of the people who work on the family estate and for those who work for the companies that operate under our corporate banner. I don't want to let any of them down by doing or saying something stupid that then hits the press and damages our businesses. That can affect people's jobs and whether they can pay their mortgage or put food on the table. It reassures me to have Simon as an adviser so that I don't balls things up.'

'We want to help, Sergeant,' Derringer said, also taking a seat. 'We'll answer any questions you put to us openly and honestly.'

'Well, I can't ask more than that, gentlemen,' Hamish said, impressed by Wade's candid attitude. 'Now, how long have you been friends wi' Darius Palmerston, Lord Carsely?'

'Congratulations on using the correct style of address, Sergeant,' Wade said. 'A lot of people get it wrong – they get confused with the whole viscount thing. I don't really care, but I feel awful for people who think they've embarrassed themselves.'

'This is no' my first brush wi' the upper crust,' Hamish said. 'So, about Palmerston . . .'

'I wouldn't say we were friends exactly,' Wade explained. 'Acquaintances is the term, I think. I choose my friends very carefully, Sergeant.'

'Mere acquaintances?' Davey said. 'Yet you came all the way up here for this wedding.'

'I may not have counted Darius as a firm friend,' Wade said, 'but I had my own reasons for wanting to come. This was Alannah's wedding, too, Constable, and we've been friends far longer than I've known Darius.'

'How did you come to know Alannah?' Hamish asked.

'We met at parties and she was part of the social scene in London,' said Wade. 'At one time, I'm pretty sure her father hoped I would be the one putting a ring on her finger. We're members of the same London club and he often dropped hints about finding his daughter "the right sort of chap". I adore Alannah but we've never really seen each other as husband and wife. I'm sort of glad about that because it's made us better friends.'

'And how did you come to meet Darius?' asked Hamish.

'He appeared on the scene about three years ago,' said Wade. 'He made a big play for Alannah and a couple of us were a little concerned about that.'

'Why concerned?' asked Davey.

'Well, no one actually knew who he was,' Wade went on. 'He seemed to appear out of nowhere with Seb in tow. He claimed to have been in the army and then done some travelling around Europe, making it sound like what gentlemen used to call "The Grand Tour".'

'You sound like you didn't believe him,' Hamish said.

'I didn't need to believe him, Sergeant.' Wade smiled and looked to Derringer. 'I don't like to take these things on faith. That's one of the many things Simon takes care of for me.'

With a nod to acknowledge that he had just been given permission to reveal private matters, Derringer spoke up.

'I ran background checks on Darius and Sebastian,' he said. 'I could find no trace of them having been in the army or any other branch of the armed forces. Darius had inherited a great deal of money and the pair of them had spent the best part of ten years swanning around the continent living a playboy lifestyle – skiing in the winter and sunning themselves on beaches around the Med in the summer.'

'All financed by his inheritance?' asked Hamish.

'It would seem so,' Derringer confirmed, 'although he did run into a few cash-flow problems latterly.'

'That all appeared to have been settled by the time he arrived in London,' Wade continued. 'He had no shortage of funds by then, but he was still an odd character, and still had poor old Seb at his elbow.'

'Did you tell Alannah that Darius was lying about his past?' Davey asked.

'Oh, yes,' Wade answered, nodding, 'but she wouldn't hear a word against him. She said she had everything under control. I thought that a strange way to talk about a relationship, but she was happy and that was all that mattered to me.'

'It came as no surprise when they got engaged, then?' Davey asked.

'It did to some,' Wade said with a short laugh. 'There were a few who thought Darius was more likely to get engaged to Seb . . . but that wasn't the nature of his relationship with Seb.'

'What was it between those two, then?' asked Hamish.

'They were like brothers, but it wasn't really a very healthy relationship, in my opinion,' Wade replied. 'Darius was the dominant one. Seb was a bit socially inept and lived completely in Darius's shadow. Simon said they led a "playboy lifestyle" in Europe, but I suspect it was Darius doing the playboy bit, with Seb very much in the background. He's certainly never been known to have a girlfriend, although I know Sloane's always been a bit sweet on him. In fact, Darius controlled him so closely I don't know how he would ever have managed any kind of relationship with a woman. He bossed him around to the extent that it could sometimes become fairly embarrassing.'

'In what way?' Davey asked.

'We've all been at weekend get-togethers when we've come in from a muddy walk in the fresh air – great hangover cure – and you pull off your wellies before going properly indoors for a coffee,' Wade said. 'Darius would plonk himself down and order Seb to haul his boots off. Seb simply went straight ahead and did as he was told. He laughed it off if anyone commented on it. He always seemed content just to be there with Darius.'

'Was Charles Hamilton happy about his daughter's choice of husband?' Hamish asked.

'He must have been,' Wade said, and smiled. 'He even got Darius into our club, although Darius might have had cause to regret that.'

'Why would that be?' Davey asked.

Wade turned to Derringer again with a questioning look. Derringer shrugged.

'It's common knowledge at the club,' he said, 'so it's no secret. They could find out anyway.'

'There's a group of us sometimes like to play a few hands of poker at the club,' Wade said. 'Naturally, there's a wager involved and Darius ended up owing me a few quid.'

'How much is a few quid?' Hamish asked.

'Twenty thousand pounds,' Wade replied.

'To most folk,' Hamish pointed out, 'that's quite a lot o' money – no' just a few quid.'

'I realise that, Sergeant,' Wade said, nodding, 'but there are also some "folk" who will lose that much in a casino in an evening and not bat an eyelid. I don't think Darius was one of those,' he added, shaking his head. 'I'm not bothered about the money. It's not like he robbed me. He didn't take money from me, but I doubt it's a debt he ever intended to honour.'

'So he owed you a pile o' money,' Hamish said gravely. 'Where were you when he was killed?'

Wade frowned and leant over to whisper in Derringer's ear. Derringer smiled, nodded and stood up.

'Excuse me, gentlemen,' he said. 'I'll be back in just a moment.'

He left the room and Hamish glowered at Wade.

'I'm no' in the mood to wait,' Hamish said. 'Where were you?'

'Actually, Sergeant, I was in a room very similar to this

but on the other side of reception, just off the bar area,' Wade said. 'It's slightly smaller and isn't much used during the winter, according to Priscilla, because it can be a quite chilly. It doesn't get any direct sunlight, you see, although it has lovely big windows that look out over the rhododendrons in the driveway. Fortunately, Priscilla had made sure there were logs burning merrily in the fireplace, so it was a cosy little spot, especially with the flowers and—'

'I don't need a complete description o' the entire décor,' Hamish said, making it clear his patience was running thin. 'What were you doing there?'

At that point, Derringer walked back into the room accompanied by Helen Carter. They paused just inside the door, Helen taking in what was going on.

'Actually, Sergeant,' Wade said, standing when Helen entered the room, 'I was down on one knee proposing marriage to the girl I love ... and she accepted.' He fished a ring box out of his pocket, flipping it open to reveal an elegant display of diamonds and sapphires on a gold band. 'Helen is such a sweetie that she wouldn't wear the ring and didn't want to tell anyone for fear of stealing Alannah's thunder on her big day.'

She ran to him, flung her arms around his neck and kissed him, then pulled away with her eyes full of tears.

'It's okay, darling,' he said, tenderly. 'It's all going to be all right.'

'No,' she said, facing Hamish with the tears now tumbling down her cheeks. 'It's Sloane.'

'What about Sloane?' Wade said, staring sternly at Hamish. 'What's wrong with Sloane? What's happened?'

Hamish took a deep breath and got to his feet, facing Wade and Helen.

'I'm sorry to say that Sloane Beaumont was murdered here in the hotel yesterday at around the same time as Darius Palmerston,' he said.

'Sloane's dead?' Wade hugged Helen close. 'Oh, Helen, I'm so sorry! You must have been going through hell. Why didn't you tell me? Why did no one tell me?' He looked up at Derringer and then Hamish.

'I knew nothing . . .' Derringer said in little more than a whisper, the shock stealing his voice.

'I ordered everyone to keep quiet about Sloane,' Hamish said. 'The longer we could keep her death a secret, the more chance I had in these interviews of spotting the killer making a slip and giving themselves away.'

'I will not be going back to my room, Sergeant, and neither will Helen,' Wade said continuing to hold her tight. 'She needs to be with me right now. We will go to the sitting room I told you about.'

'That's fine, sir,' Hamish said. 'You two should be together. I'm sorry all o' this has spoiled what should have been such a happy time for both o' you.'

'We have many happy times ahead,' Wade said, looking into Helen's eyes. 'A whole lifetime of them. We'll get through this together.'

She pulled away from him slightly, reached for his hand and took the ring box from him. Without a word, she put the ring on her finger and they left the room arm-in-arm.

'Well, um . . . I'll go back to the room, Sergeant,' Derringer said. 'I don't think he needs me in that meeting.'

'Right you are, Mr Derringer,' Hamish said, suddenly feeling exhausted. With Derringer gone, he then said to Davey: 'Could you give me a minute, Davey? I need some time to think.'

Davey left the room, heading for the kitchen with a rumbling stomach to check out the sandwich situation. Hamish lowered himself into his chair, leaning back and staring at the ceiling. He traced the intricate patterns of the Victorian ceiling rose with his eyes, then let them flit around the room following the myriad forms of vine leaves, fruit and flowers in the plasterwork of the cornicing. So delicate. So pretty. So easily broken.

He thought of Sloane Beaumont – beautiful, lively and full of fun. Who could have brought themselves to smash her head in? Who would have wanted to snuff out that sparkling life? He reached into his pocket to retrieve the envelope of her mementos, opening the flap and leaning forward to spill the contents onto the table.

There was a handful of postcards from holiday spots, although the cards hadn't been written or sent. Presumably these were souvenirs from places Sloane had visited. There were also three photographs of the size you might keep in a wallet.

He looked for Sloane in the photographs, but she wasn't there. He assumed these must be friends or relatives. One picture showed a woman with a long-haired, bearded man sitting together at a table outside a bar in the sunshine. Both were wearing sunglasses and smiling for the camera. He flipped it over and written on the back was the word 'Nice' and a date that placed it five years ago.

The second photo showed the same couple standing on the quayside at a marina with an array of luxury yachts forming the backdrop. Again, the sky was blue and both were wearing dark glasses. On the reverse were the words 'Cannes' and again the photo was five years old.

The final picture featured the same man, again sitting smiling in the sunshine but this time with a platter of seafood and glasses of white wine on the table in front of him, and the woman was missing, replaced by a male companion, both again wearing dark glasses. On the reverse, it was tagged 'St Tropez' and also dated five years ago.

In a way, Hamish was glad that Sloane hadn't kept any photos of herself among her envelope of treasures. At that moment, he didn't really want such a stark reminder of the girl who had been flirting with him just two days before and made him blush. It would be easier to think of her as an anonymous victim. That way he could be completely objective and keep his thoughts in order. He shook his head, the idea of trying to dismiss her personality feeling utterly disrespectful. Darius Palmerston wasn't someone he'd enjoyed being around, but Sloane had been. She'd been fun and, as people had been telling him, always at the centre of things. He frowned – so why wasn't she in any of those photos?

He examined the pictures again and, with the creeping chill of dreadful realisation, he finally recognised the woman. The images of the men, too, then took on a haunting familiarity. The reason that Sloane wasn't in any of the photos was that these were not her photos.

'Silas!' Hamish yelled, stomping over to yank open the door. 'Get Alannah Hamilton down here now!'

He clumped back to his seat and slammed himself down into it, thinking hard. This whole weekend – the wedding and everything surrounding it – had been a bizarre game, and the name of the game was 'Control'. Wade had mentioned the word a couple of times, and folk scheming for control was what had created this entire nightmare.

Darius had been controlling Seb for years and did it because it was his nature. For the other players in the game, control was their goal, but something had gone disastrously wrong and he was teetering on the brink of understanding what that was. He could think of only one person who would be able to explain.

'Did you want to speak to me, Sergeant?' Alannah said in a strained voice, walking meekly into the room.

'Sit down, Alannah,' Hamish instructed her and she sat on the very edge of the seat opposite him, staring at him with large, watery eyes.

'I hope you don't want to ask me lots of exhausting questions,' she said wearily. 'I feel totally wiped out. I really don't feel up to an interrogation.'

'This doesn't have to be an interrogation,' Hamish said, 'but you have to answer my questions truthfully.'

'If you have lots of questions,' Alannah said, 'then I'd feel happier with someone here to help me. Maybe you could ask Helen to come in . . . or Sloane.'

'Cut the crap, Alannah,' Hamish said. 'I ken you're upset, but I think you're fully aware that Sloane's no' coming to help you, and you ken why. In fact, you're one o' the people who understands exactly what's been going on here this weekend.'

'I . . . I don't know what you mean,' Alannah said.

'Aye, but you do,' Hamish retorted. 'The bride is at the centre o' any wedding, and you've been right at the heart o' everything that's happened in the past twenty-four hours and beyond, haven't you?'

'No, you're not making sense—' Alannah began but was interrupted when the door burst open and her father thundered in.

'What the hell do you think you're doing, Macbeth?!'

he yelled, pointing at Hamish. 'How dare you drag my daughter down here when she's barely able to . . .'

Charles Hamilton paused and froze, as though he had forgotten what he was about to say. Beads of sweat broke out on his brow and cheeks and he clenched his teeth in an agonised grimace. His right hand flew to his chest and he collapsed backwards into the metal cabinet before slumping to the floor.

Chapter Ten

> *Love will subsist on wonderfully little hope but not altogether without it.*
>
> Sir Walter Scott, *Waverley* (1814)

'He needs to take one of his tablets!' Alannah said, crouching over her father and fumbling through his jacket pockets. Hamish stooped to help, finding a small bottle of pills in the first pocket he tried.

Alannah took one of the tablets, opened her father's mouth and popped the pill under his tongue.

'He's having an angina attack,' she explained. 'I've seen this before. The tablet will relieve the pain in just a couple of minutes.'

'I'll send for Dr Brodie,' Silas said from the doorway, fishing his phone out of his pocket.

As Alannah predicted, her father's symptoms had eased dramatically by the time the doctor arrived. He examined Hamilton and judged it safe to move his patient through to the bar area where he could be made more comfortable. Hamish and Silas gently lifted Hamilton and carried him through reception to where Dr Brodie made sure they propped him up comfortably on a sofa. He then sat in a chair beside him, checking his pulse and temperature just as he had done in the incident room. By then, Hamilton was beginning to complain about the unwanted attention.

'That's a good sign,' Alannah said, with a flicker of a smile. 'He must be starting to feel better if he's able to moan about being fussed over.'

'That's grand,' Hamish said, standing back with Alannah to give Dr Brodie space to work. Serena Hamilton then arrived and rushed to her husband's side. Alannah curled her lip at the sight of her stepmother fawning over her father.

'Let's leave him wi' Silas and the doctor, Alannah,' Hamish said. 'We can carry on wi' our wee chat in the incident room.'

'Sloane . . .' Alannah said as soon as Hamish closed the incident-room door behind them. 'How did she . . . ?'

'She was hit in the back o' the head,' Hamish said, crossing to his seat. 'She wouldn't have felt a thing. We've no' found any murder weapon yet. My bet is it was chucked outside and is buried under the snow.'

Alannah lowered herself into her chair, staring at the table.

'I knew as soon as I found Darius's body that something must have happened to Sloane,' she said. 'Then, when she didn't come to see me and no one would tell me where she was . . . I knew she must be dead . . . and . . . and it was all my fault.'

'What do you mean?' Hamish asked.

'She was trying to help me.'

'How?'

'I knew Serena and Darius were having an affair,' Alannah said. 'I wanted to tell Daddy, but I didn't have any real proof. Sloane thought she could find proof.'

'How did she intend to do that?'

'She hated the way Darius treated Seb. She thought Seb was really quite cute and just needed a little encouragement to come out of his shell and stand on his own two feet. Sloane said she thought he liked her and that she could persuade him to come up with something we could use against Darius.'

'You were plotting against the man you married in the church yesterday!' Hamish had known it was true, but still found it abhorrent.

'I *needed* to get married! It was the only way that . . .'

'Aye, I ken about the inheritance. I'm also fully aware o' your relationship wi' Paul Hunter. If you needed to get married, why did you no' just marry him?'

'Daddy would never have allowed that. Paul was not the sort of man he wanted me to marry. He could never have become part of the business. He's not remotely interested in money or finance or investments, but Daddy had to agree to my choice of husband for the marriage to trigger the inheritance.'

'So your plan was to marry Darius, then expose his affair wi' Serena. Your father would then deal wi' both o' them however he saw fit and you would be able to divorce Darius.'

'There could be no divorce,' Alannah said, taking a deep breath. 'It was one of the inheritance stipulations – no divorce within five years. The money comes to me in two parts and the second instalment would simply go to my father if I divorced Darius. In the meantime, Paul and I would have enough to start building our life together and Daddy wouldn't be able to stop us. We'd just have to wait five years for the rest of the money or to get married.'

'Unless you killed Darius,' Hamish reasoned.

'I hated him,' she said, gritting her teeth, 'but I never planned to kill him.'

'No, I don't think you did,' Hamish said. 'You didn't plan to kill him, but I don't think his murder was planned. It happened in a split second, and you were the one who came out o' that room covered in blood.'

'No!' she cried. 'I just found him lying there! I knelt down to see if he was still alive. That's how I got blood on me. You have to believe me!'

'I don't have to *believe* anything,' Hamish told her. 'I have to find hard evidence – proof o' guilt or innocence, and right now the evidence is leaning towards you and Paul having lost control. The situation got out o' your hands and the result was the deaths o' your husband and your best friend.'

'That's all nonsense! We had no reason to want Sloane to die!'

'But plenty o' reason to want Darius dead.'

'You've got it wrong, Sergeant Macbeth.' Alannah leant forward, looking straight at Hamish, her eyes imploring him to believe her. 'Paul and I aren't killers. We could never do something like that.'

'Aye, maybe,' Hamish said, nodding thoughtfully. 'I think the truth's about to come out. Then we'll see.'

Hamish showed Alannah out and she stood in reception, glaring across into the bar where Serena was sitting by her father's side. Serena slowly turned her head and fixed Alannah with an unblinking stare, the hint of a cruel smile playing at the corners of her painted lips.

'She thinks she's won . . .' Alannah said in a faint whisper. 'Perhaps she has.'

She then headed up the main staircase and Dr Brodie crossed the floor to talk to Hamish.

'It really is beginning to feel like I should just move in here,' he said, shaking his head, then pointing towards Hamilton. 'That man, however, can't stay here. He needs to be properly monitored in hospital, the sooner the better.'

'He might have to wait,' Hamish said. 'We've no way to . . .'

His voice trailed off as there came rhythmic vibration that turned into the now familiar beat of a helicopter's rotor blades. They walked through to the window in the incident room to watch a black-and-yellow Police Scotland helicopter drifting down to land on the same spot Richard Jensen's machine had used three days earlier, sending up a similar cloud of misty spindrift.

'Looks like we've got a ride for Mr Hamilton after all,' Hamish said and they hurried outside.

Silas was already standing by the landing site when Hamish and Dr Brodie got there. He denied having had anything to do with the helicopter's arrival, then one of the aircraft's doors opened and, to Hamish's surprise, out stepped DCI Jimmy Anderson. Hamish stomped through the snow to greet him. Jimmy looked almost as white as the snow.

'I promised myself I'd never get back in one o' yon whirlybirds again,' he said, recalling that his only previous experience had left him feeling like he'd spent a week on a rollercoaster. 'Get me to the bar, Hamish. I need a dram.'

'I thought you were off the sauce, Jimmy,' Hamish said, the memory of finding his friend lying injured at the side of the road after having crashed his car fleeting through his mind.

'One quick swally to steady me, then we can get down to business,' Jimmy said.

Serena Hamilton was still sitting with her husband when they entered the bar. The doctor went to check on his patient and Hamish explained that Charles Hamilton needed to go to the hospital in Braikie. Jimmy agreed to organise that, sipping his whisky at the bar.

'When the top brass heard this was a double murder and that Daviot was out o' action,' he explained, 'they sent that thing outside up from Glasgow to bring me here and take charge. It can do a wee hop to Braikie wi' Hamilton and the doctor on its way home.'

Minutes later, Hamish and Jimmy were standing in the incident room watching the helicopter disappear off towards Braikie with Dr Brodie and Charles Hamilton on board.

'Okay, Hamish,' Jimmy said, sitting at the table and pouring himself a mug of coffee from a pot Silas had supplied, 'fill me in on where you've got to.'

Hamish explained about Paul Hunter's attempted escape, the bloodied clothes they'd found and gave Jimmy a rough breakdown of each of the conversations he'd had in that room.

'I've spoken to nearly all the main suspects we've identified so far,' Hamish said. 'I've run through so many scenarios in my mind that my heid's fair buzzing. The main thing is that, whoever murdered Darius Palmerston would have been able to get into the breakfast room from outside, from the upper floors using the backstairs or from the kitchen corridor. Darius must also have used one o' those routes because he wasn't seen going in there from the dining room – nobody knew where he was.

'The killer must then have left the same way he or she came into the room. Wi' access to the whole hotel, they can then go upstairs to get cleaned up and no' be seen leaving the breakfast room wi' bloodstained clothes.'

'Which is exactly what Alannah Hamilton did,' Jimmy said.

'Aye, and since nobody else was in the breakfast room when she says she discovered the body, that looks bad for her,' Hamish agreed. 'Maybe she has motive and opportunity for Palmerston's murder, but I can't see why she would want to kill Sloane Beaumont. There's so much more going on here, Jimmy – loads o' scheming and plotting – but there's one last interview I'd like to do that will help us get to the bottom o' it all.'

'Fair enough,' Jimmy said. 'You know these folk and what they've told you so far. You take the lead and I'll back you up if you need it.'

Hamish went out into reception and asked Silas to bring Sebastian Chalmers down to the incident room, then went back to wait with Jimmy.

'He's a bit odd, Jimmy,' Hamish explained, 'but if we handle him right we'll get the truth out o' him.'

Silas showed Chalmers in and Hamish introduced him to Jimmy.

'I know you've been through a lot ower the past twenty-four hours, Seb,' Hamish said, trying to keep the tone as friendly as possible, 'but we'd like to learn as much as we can about Darius, and you were his closest friend. The more we ken about Darius, the more likely we are to find something that will help us prove who killed him.'

'I heard you had Paul Hunter locked up for the murders,' Sebastian said.

'Did you now?' Hamish replied, nodding. 'Well, it's true that we have Paul in custody and things are no' looking good for him, but we're no' quite ready to charge him wi' murder yet. Maybe you'll be able to tell us something that changes that.'

'I'll do what I can, to help,' Sebastian said.

'Good,' Hamish began, 'so when did you first meet Darius?'

'We met at school. My father sent me away to bloody boarding school when I was barely eleven.'

'I take it you weren't too keen on going?'

'I was terrified by the whole thing. I'd never really been away from home before. He said it would toughen me up.' Sebastian laughed without any humour, clearly finding the whole concept of the school toughening him up absurd.

'Why did he think you needed toughening up?'

'Because I'd been to four different day schools by the time I was nine years old. Eventually, my father's patience ran out. He saw me as a burden and wanted me out of his life, so he sent me off to boarding school.'

'That's an odd way for a father to treat his son.'

'You'd think so, wouldn't you? Fathers are supposed to love their sons, cherish them and support them. I had none of that from my father. He detested me.'

'Why was that?'

'Because my mother died in childbirth, Sergeant. She died giving me life. Growing up, I never had a mother. I'm not even sure what she looked like. My father got rid of any photos and became very angry if I ever asked about her. I think he must have loved her a great deal. He certainly didn't love me. He blamed me for her death and any love, tenderness or compassion in the man died with her.'

'What about your grandparents? Weren't they able to help try to give you a better upbringing?'

'When I was a baby, I'm sure they must have, but my father moved house and kept them at arm's length after that. Then the torture of school began.'

'What made your first schools so bad?'

'I don't think they were bad schools as such, but I was awkward with other kids. I found it difficult to mix. I preferred being on my own. Other kids didn't like me and if there was any trouble it was always blamed on me.'

'What sort of trouble?'

'Anything from a broken window to graffiti or a bin being set on fire – I got the blame. A teacher's purse was stolen once and everyone pointed the finger at me. Of course, I never did any of that stuff, but I was the easiest to blame. I was shy and didn't know how to talk to people. I didn't wear the same sort of clothes as the other kids because my father bought what he considered "proper" clothes, which meant I always looked about twenty years behind the times. They teased me for that. They teased me for being different and as time went by I was bullied mercilessly. Do you know what it's like to be different, Sergeant? Do you know what it's like always to be an outsider?'

'Aye, I've an idea what that can be like,' Hamish replied.

He thought of all the people he'd encountered over the years who had come to Sutherland seeking an idyllic lifestyle, farming a croft, living off the land and leaving the cares of city life behind. None had the least idea about how cruel the elements could be in the far northwest of Scotland. Protecting your home and livestock, let alone any crops you might grow, from the savage wind and lashing rain in winter was a never-ending task. Worse still for some was the fact that the heavy cloud during such a storm meant they might not see proper daylight for days on end.

Most of those who made it through the first winter were gone by the time the second set in. Many of the rest simply drank themselves into oblivion, yet those who had the tenacity to stay, even those befriended by the local community, were forever considered to be outsiders. Hamish himself, having been born and brought up in Rogart on the other side of Sutherland, knew he was seen as an outsider by many of the locals born in Lochdubh. He'd experienced their jealousy when they saw him living in a house they thought was better than theirs; when they saw him driving around in a Land Rover they could never afford; when they read about a police pay rise in the papers – and they bitched about it all being paid for by them when the taxman took their money. He'd had to work hard to win them over but knew that, for some, he'd remain an outsider till the day he died.

'Do you really, Sergeant? Do you know what it's like to feel utterly alone, banished from your home by a father who hates the very sight of you? That boarding school was hell for me. Do you know what it's like to be bullied and beaten up by a bunch of vicious little bastards just for their amusement? They used to strip me naked and lock me out of the dormitory in the freezing rain. They used to piss in my bed and smear shit in my books and if I said a word about it to anyone, I could look forward to another beating ... or worse. Many times I thought about ending it all – killing myself – but I never had the guts.' He paused for a second, shaking his head and rubbing his temples.

'And then along came Darius,' he went on, blinking and sniffing to clear his thoughts. 'He was just another new boy as far as the others were concerned, but he didn't take any crap from anyone. The first time they tried ganging up on him, he went berserk. He punched the ringleader's front teeth out and broke another's wrist with a tennis racquet. When he realised what they'd been doing to me, he told me he'd look after me. He stuck up for me. He was always there by my side and the rest of them just left us alone.'

'So you two have been best pals ever since you were at boarding school?'

'Yes. Once Darius and I became friends I rarely saw my father again. Even during the school holidays, I didn't go home. Darius took me home with him. His parents didn't mind. He told them I was an orphan, which might as well have been true.'

'I believe his parents died in an accident?'

'That was a day I'll never forget. We were both eighteen and had just finished our final term at that damned school. Our bags were packed and we were ready to leave. We'd decided we would join the army and maybe see a bit of the world. We were looking forward to a lazy summer before we signed up. Darius's parents were on their way to pick us up, but they never arrived.'

'Darius must have been devastated.'

'We both were. I'd come to look on them as my surrogate parents and I was totally gutted when they died, but it was worse for Darius. He was in a complete daze. He told me he didn't know how he would have got through it without me. After the funeral we decided there was nothing to keep us at home, so we went down to the recruiting office and signed up.'

'You joined the army?' Hamish asked, looking for absolute clarity.

'That's right,' Sebastian replied, staring down at his hands fidgeting on the table.

'Aye, but it's no' right, really, is it?' Hamish objected. 'There's no record o' either o' you ever having been in the army and Darius's claims about having been an officer in the Household Cavalry were shot full o' holes by Colonel Halburton-Smythe who, unlike you and Darius, really was a military man. So why lie about the army?'

'It was Darius's idea,' Sebastian said. 'It's a lie we've been telling for so long, I've kind of come to believe it myself. He said people wouldn't come looking for us if we told them we were in the army.'

'And why would people come looking for you?'

'I suppose Darius's cousins, Stephen and Henry, have told you that he stole all the family money?' Chalmers said.

'Something like that,' Hamish agreed.

'Well, it was his parents' money, so it was his by rights. He couldn't be bothered with a bunch of gold diggers pestering us, so he said we should pretend to have disappeared into the army.'

'What did you do instead?'

'We went travelling. We went all round Europe and enjoyed ourselves. When we started to run low on funds, we came home.'

'Were you perhaps more than just a wee bit low on funds?'

'I'm not sure what you mean,' Sebastian said, staring at his hands again. To Hamish, it was a sure sign he was lying. 'Darius took care of all the money.'

'I'm sure he did,' Hamish said, 'but I think you know more than you're saying. However, we'll pass over that wee lie for now. So you came home to London, and then Darius met Alannah Hamilton.'

'That's right,' Sebastian agreed. 'We used to see her at parties and in nightclubs. Before long they were dating and became engaged.'

'Can you remember when you first met her father and stepmother?' Hamish asked.

'Probably at one of those weekend parties at her place in the country,' Sebastian said, and Hamish got the impression he was consciously trying not to stare down at his hands.

'So you've known them for what – two or three years?'

'About that.'

'How do you get on with Serena Hamilton?'

'I don't really know her that well at all,' Sebastian said, sitting up straight, gripping the arms of his chair. 'Seldom even spoke to her.'

'Darius knew her pretty well, though, didn't he?'

'I . . . I'm not sure what you're implying . . .'

'What about Alannah's friends? Did you get on wi' them? What about Sloane?'

'Sloane was really fun. I liked her a lot,' Sebastian said, staring off into space.

'"Was"? "Liked"? Why are you talking about her in the past tense?'

'I . . . don't know . . . because I saw her yesterday.'

'When was the last time you saw her?'

'Um . . . at the wedding meal.'

'Where were you when Darius was killed?'

'I went up to our room . . . to use the toilet.'

'There's a gents down here just past reception.'

'I . . . I won't use public lavatories.'

'What does this message mean?' Hamish held up his iPad showing an image of the 'SHE KNOWS' text. 'Why did you send it to Darius on the morning of his wedding?'

'He planned to take Alannah out riding in the snow today as a surprise,' Sebastian said, staring at his hands, which were back on the table, 'but she found out. Paul told her.'

'Very good, Seb,' Hamish congratulated him. 'Did you just think o' that or have you been rehearsing it ever since you realised that we would find the message on your phone?'

'I . . . no, I mean . . .' Sebastian stumbled over his words.

'That's enough, laddie,' Hamish said. 'That was a lot o' questions and so many lies from you that I've lost count o' them. So, instead o' you trying to tell me another pack o' lies, I'm going to tell you what happened.

'When you and Darius went travelling, you blew his entire fortune living the high life and then started lying, cheating and stealing to carry on doing the same. Then things changed.'

Hamish produced the envelope Helen had given him, fanned out the postcards on the table and placed the three photographs side-by-side.

'These are yours, aren't they?' he said.

'Yes, I . . . how did you get these?' Sebastian was horrified. 'These are my souvenirs, my little treasures. I carry them everywhere.'

'I'm sure you do,' Hamish said. 'This photo,' he continued, pointing to the one of the two men, 'if you look past the sunglasses, long hair and suchlike, is you and

Darius in the south of France. I'd say it was probably taken by the woman in these two photos. That's Darius with Serena Hamilton. You probably took those two, but the pictures are all from five years ago. You've known Serena far longer than you said.

'My bet is that Serena was on her own in France and Darius got chatting to her. Maybe at first he saw her as someone you two could rip off, but she wasn't about to be hoodwinked by the likes o' you. She's a wily operator and saw right through you. She hit it off wi' Darius, though, and that's where their affair started. Given that you seemed to treat Darius as some kind o' father figure, I think you maybe saw them together as an ideal couple – your own wee happy family.

'The south o' France is also where Darius and Serena started planning for the future. Serena was looking for a way to take control o' the Hamilton fortune. She wanted to be sitting on all that money wi' Darius at her side but they needed a way to get you two back to England and let her carry on seeing him until Charles eventually died or became so ill he could no longer run the business. Wi' his heart condition and the way he smoked, drank and worried, they reckoned they wouldn't have long to wait. Some o' Charles's money and property, however, was bound to go to Alannah, and Serena didn't want that.

'Then Serena discovered that Alannah would have a separate inheritance if she married – a fortune that had nothing to do wi' Charles. She also discovered that Alannah was in love wi' Paul, but would never be allowed to marry him. Charles wanted her to have a husband he could bring into the family business and control. Paul was way too low down the social scale for that but Serena could see that Alannah desperately wanted to be wi' him. She then asked herself what she would do in Alannah's position and the answer was simple – find a disposable husband, one she could marry for the money and then abandon.

'If Alannah did that, she would take the inheritance due on her marriage and run away wi' Paul, leaving Serena and Darius free to start prizing the business out o' Charles's hands. How am I doing so far, Seb?'

Sebastian stared at Hamish, looking very uncomfortable.

'Serena shipped you and Darius back to England and he worked on establishing his playboy image,' Hamish went on. 'Priscilla was one o' his conquests. Serena engineered the initial meetings between Alannah and Darius so that he could start romancing her. Although she didn't know she was being played, this was fine by Alannah, who thought she'd found her disposable husband. This was working well for all concerned until Alannah discovered that Darius was having an affair with Serena. It wouldn't have taken her long to then realise that Serena had set her up wi' Darius and to figure out their long-term plan.

'The idea o' Darius and Serena taking over the family business, and using her to do so, appalled Alannah. All she needed to stop them was proof o' the affair, and that really brings us to this weekend, doesn't it, Seb? Sloane thought she could help Alannah by finding proof. She liked you, Seb. She thought you could make something o' yourself if you just climbed out o' Darius's pocket. I think you liked her, too, didn't you, Seb?'

Sebastian nodded and let his chin drop to his chest with what sounded like it might have been a sob. That was it. That was what Hamish had been looking for.

Now he knew how to get to Sebastian. Sloane was the key.

'Sloane came to your room to have a wee heart-to-heart wi' you some time yesterday morning. Maybe Darius even gave you the room, thinking you two could enjoy some time alone together. While she was in there, Sloane managed to steal this envelope and the photos that prove Serena and Darius were long-term lovers. When you discovered it was gone, you texted Darius the "SHE KNOWS" message.

'Darius now knew he had a problem. After the wedding, he got you to lure Sloane back up to your room for another talk, but this time he was there, too. There was an argument and Darius lost his temper. Poor Sloane – so much fun, so full of life, such a dazzling young beauty. She never knew what hit her, did she? What was it, Seb? What was it that ended Sloane's life? What was it Darius used to smash Sloane's skull in?'

'It was a vase!' Chalmers shouted, suddenly animated. 'It was one of those heavy crystal flower vases! He whacked her with base of it and she fell on the rug, and . . .'

'Okay, Seb,' Hamish said. 'What did he do with it?'

'He wiped it with a towel and threw it out the window into the garden.'

'And it disappeared into the snow,' Hamish said. 'You both then cleaned up a bit, rolled Sloane in the rug and put her in the broom cupboard, but you weren't at all happy about that, were you, Seb?'

'We walked down the backstairs. We were arguing.' Sebastian's voice dropped to a whisper and he was visibly tensing up, as though reliving the moment. 'Darius and Serena treated their relationship and the marriage as one big joke. She even sent him a Valentine's card on the morning of the wedding and he thought it was hilarious. I told him he should be grateful for that . . . a token of love . . . and he laughed again and tore it up right in front of me.

'It took a while for it to sink in after he killed Sloane, then I got really angry. I told him he shouldn't have done that. I said it wasn't fair that he got to be married and to have a lover and I was left out in the cold. He'd killed the only woman who ever cared about me! By now we were in the breakfast room. He told me not to be so stupid. He said Sloane was never interested in me and called me pathetic! I picked up the sword and—'

Sebastian jumped to his feet, his right arm raised high. Hamish pushed his seat back, ready to restrain him but Sebastian dropped back into his seat, put his face in his hands and wept.

'You had blood on your clothes,' Hamish said. 'You ran back upstairs and got changed, stuffed the kilt outfit into a plastic carrier bag and headed out to the back of the hotel. You were out in the snow, trying to think of somewhere to hide the clothes, when you saw Paul Hunter running towards the hotel. He'd heard something had happened and was trying to get to Alannah. He didn't spot you, but you knew his bedsit would now be empty. You sneaked in there, smeared his uniform with blood from your own clothes and left them under a blanket at the bottom of his wardrobe where you knew a simple search would find them. You thought that would make Paul the prime suspect for the murders.

'You then went back out into the snow and hid your own clothes under one of the sheds where you hoped they might never be found. That's how it all happened, isn't it, Seb?'

'Yes,' Sebastian looked up, his face stained with tears. 'Darius killed Sloane and I lost my head and did that to him with the sword.'

Hamish let out a deep breath and sat back in his chair, exhausted. Jimmy stood up, walked round the table.

'Stand up, please, laddie,' he said to Sebastian, then produced a set of handcuffs and slapped them on his wrists. 'I am Detective Chief Inspector James Anderson. Sebastian Chalmers, I am arresting you for murder . . .' Jimmy recited the arrest mantra, then turned to Hamish. 'We need to take him into custody. We can release Paul Hunter and this one will take his place in your cell at the station.'

'Aye, Jimmy,' Hamish said, heaving himself to his feet. 'Let's go.'

They got as far as the door, Jimmy holding Sebastian's upper left arm and Hamish following immediately behind him, when Sebastian stopped and turned to look at them both.

'I'm sorry,' he said quietly, then he dipped his shoulder into Jimmy's chest, knocking him backwards into Hamish. A police officer standing by the hotel entrance took a step towards him and Sebastian dashed for the main staircase, his hands still cuffed in front of him.

Hamish was past Jimmy in an instant and off up the stairs after Sebastian with Silas and the officer from the front door at his heels. They had still not caught up with Sebastian by the time they reached the second floor and could hear his footsteps pounding on up to the top of the hotel. They followed on and found another officer, who had been patrolling the corridor, waiting for them.

'He went in there,' the officer said, pointing to the door that led out onto the roof.

'Damn!' Silas said, panting for breath. 'I must have forgotten to lock it!'

Hamish climbed the short flight of steps to the roof and looked out to where Sebastian was standing, balanced precariously on Tommel Castle's mock battlements, snow beneath his shoes and a deadly drop in front of him.

'Seb,' Hamish said calmly, 'come down from there. There's no need for this.'

'Yes, there is,' Sebastian said, his shoulders heaving with huge sobs. 'There's nothing left for me. I can't spend the rest of my life in prison. Boarding school was bad enough . . . but prison . . .'

'It won't be the rest o' your life, Seb,' Hamish said. 'You did what you did while the balance o' your mind was disturbed – that's how they'll see it. You'd been coerced, controlled and mentally abused for years. None o' that was your fault. You'll be able to get help to come to terms wi' it all.'

'And what then?' Sebastian sniffed. 'What sort of future do I have?'

'Sebastian Edward Chalmers,' a voice boomed up from way down on the ground. Chalmers looked down and Hamish craned his neck to see over the battlements to where a bearded figure in a kaftan was holding his arms aloft. The seer spoke again, 'Life does not end here for you. There is much for you yet to achieve and those who await you in the future will need your guidance. Step down. Now is not your time.'

Sebastian looked dazed. He stepped back, slipped and was caught by Hamish, who helped him onto the stairs. Silas took over as Sebastian walked meekly down and Hamish glanced back over the battlements, but Angus Macdonald was nowhere to be seen.

'What will happen now?' Silas asked, watching two uniformed officers lead Sebastian away down the main staircase.

'He'll stand trial, but I think they'll be lenient wi' him, given the circumstances,' Hamish said.

'And Alannah, Paul . . . the Hamiltons?' Silas said.

'That's for them to sort out themselves,' Hamish said, 'but Charles Hamilton's going to have a hard time playing down all the scandal we've seen here this weekend. What I want to know is, how the hell did auld Angus ken Seb's middle name was Edward? And how did he ken we'd be up there at that exact moment?'

A few days later, once all the fuss had died down and the snow had melted to a nuisance of slushy pavements and flooded fields, Hamish and Claire sat in the Piper, enjoying an evening together. The wedding band, having missed out on performing in the Tommel Castle Hotel had been entertaining the locals in the pub for the past three nights. Their Blues Mobile had failed to start and even Dougie Tennant couldn't fix the problem until specially ordered parts arrived.

At a table in a corner where they could enjoy the band but could also still hear each other without raising their voices, Hamish and Claire were able to relax and chat, swapping stories about everything that had happened over the past few days.

Claire told him about the woman who had called for an ambulance because she said she couldn't walk. They had showed up expecting to deal with a traumatic injury, but it turned out she'd put her boots on the wrong feet and couldn't get them off.

Because Superintendent Daviot had made a complete recovery and was not expected to experience any further ill effects, Hamish felt able to laugh with her about the strange yet urgent waddle he'd performed on his way to the gents in Tommel Castle.

'Charles Hamilton ended up in Braikie Hospital in the same ward as Daviot – their beds were next to each other,' Hamish said. 'Daviot says Alannah came to see him wi' Paul and gave her father the whole story. He was furious wi' Serena – Alannah had to calm him down. Serena was sent on her way back down south by train, and Charles told her that her bags would be packed when she got home. He got on the phone and stopped her credit cards and shut down her bank accounts as well. If she thought it was chilly up here, she's really out in the cold down there.'

'That's no more than she deserves,' Claire said. 'What about Alannah and Paul?'

'Well, Charles had just been given another reminder that his ticker's no' in good shape,' Hamish said. 'He decided that life was too short no' to make the most o' your chances to be happy. He gave Alannah and Paul his blessing. They can now start planning their future together and Alannah will join her father in the family business.'

They talked about when they might reschedule their Valentine's trip to Kylesku; the wild deer that had gone strolling down Braikie High Street; the summer dress Claire had bought in a sale even though she wouldn't get to wear it for months; they talked about friends, family, and they rekindled distant memories. Eventually, when they'd paused for a moment to sip their drinks, Hamish looked at her across the table and smiled.

'You know, wi' yon fancy wedding at Tommel Castle, and then Richard Wade getting engaged to Helen,' he said, 'and Charles Hamilton talking about how life's too short . . . I was thinking that maybe we . . . you and I . . . should possibly think about—'

Claire squealed and raced round the table before he could say another word. She dumped herself in his lap, threw her arms round his neck and kissed him.

'Hamish Macbeth,' she said with a huge grin. 'I was told the other day that you were "a keeper", but I didn't need to be told that. I've known that ever since we drove up to Kylesku in yon fancy Jaguar you'd borrowed. I think about you every second we're apart. I worry about you wi' everything that happens in your job. I love you wi' all my heart – I really do. I would marry you at the drop o' a hat. I would marry you in an instant. I would marry you in a church, on a mountainside, on a boat or up a tree for that matter . . . but I'll no' marry you just yet.

'The big wedding and Richard Wade wi' his bonny new fiancée – I saw them in the paper – all that might make you want to hear more wedding bells but that doesn't mean it's the right time for us.

'I ken fine the heartaches you've been through in the past, and I've had a couple myself, so let's wait until the dust settles, or the snow melts, and we'll both feel it when the time's right. In the meantime, you're still a keeper and I'm for keeping you . . . and you've no idea how happy it makes me to know that you feel the same about me. I'm ower the moon. You've made me feel so happy!'

She took his face in her hands and kissed him again.

'Now, come on!' She stood and took his hand. 'There's folk up dancing and I love this song!'

'Och, I'm no' really one for the dancing . . .' he said, hesitating.

She posed with a perfect pout of mock petulance, never letting go of his hand.

'In that case,' she said, 'I might have to take back everything I just said.'

'Aye, well,' he said, beaming at her, 'we can't have that, can we?'

He followed her out to join the throng of dancers crowding the middle of the pub floor knowing that no one else in the room, no one else in Lochdubh, no one else in the whole of Scotland could possibly be feeling as ridiculously in love as he was right then.

Agatha Raisin: Sugar and Spite

By M.C. Beaton
With R.W. Green

Feathers are flying in Agatha Raisin's brand new case!

Agatha Raisin can think of nothing duller than a lecture on birdwatching . . . but events take a thrilling turn when an angry interloper storms the stage at the Carsely Ladies' Society and threatens the three bird fanatics.

When Agatha later walks in on the trio of women in the middle of a blazing row, her detective instincts start 'twitching'. And when one of the birdwatchers is found dead, she can't resist investigating.

Her first lead comes from the victim's brother, who believes his sister was murdered by her fellow twitchers. Further digging reveals the disturbing nature of the women's friendship, and a bewilderingly long list of suspects.

Agatha will have to break out her binoculars and embrace her bitter side to solve the murders. Will she be able to gather all the breadcrumbs and put together the clues before she becomes a sitting duck herself?